CONNECTED BY BLOOD & KEYS

CONNECTED
BY
BLOOD & KEYS

T. J. SMITH

READ ❧ RIBBON
PUBLISHING GROUP

Text Copyright © 2024 by Theophulis Smith Jr.
Jacket Artwork © 2024 by T. J. SMITH LLC

All rights reserved. Published in the United States by Read Ribbon Publishing Group

Library of Congress Cataloging-in-Publication Data is available upon request. ISBN 978-0-9985522-5-5 (enhanced hardcover)
ISBN 978-0-9985522-8-6 (paperback)
ISBN 978-0-9985522-4-8 (ebook)

First Edition, 2024

Editor: Tara Gilboy
Cover & Interior Designer: Untoucht LLC
Illustrator: Poyjeee

Read Ribbon Publishing Group
10102 S. Redwood Rd. #95533
South Jordan, UT, 84095

www.readribbon.com

*For Rion, Shariah, and Donald. Those
we've loved, lost, and continue to live for.*

g•b•u•ni•verse

All existing matter and space considered as a
whole, a cosmos. Believed to be at least 10 billion
light years in diameter, containing a vast number of
worlds and timelines. **Ever expanding**.

PART I

PROEM

Create. Destroy. Protect. The keys to the power of The Source. Gifted in nature but isolated in existence. The Source birthed a universe of creations through power and blood. Filling the void with an array of life, but this did not satisfy the chasm. The Source decided to relinquish its power and bestow gifts to three daughters: Asha, the gift of creation, Ahnae, the peculiar gift of destruction, and Aniia, the gift of protection.

Thus, the physical form of the Source was ended.

Filled with gratitude for their creator's sacrifice, the eldest daughter, Asha, and her sisters continued to bring life to the cosmos. Destined to be the Original Mothers, Asha spawned the first new generation of gifted blood. Harboring the blood from the mother of Creation and the strands of power from the Source, the gifted bloodline became royalty. **Vasilikós**.

However, gifted blood cannot be contained. In each generation, an anomaly was born in the form of Gemini—the Connected Key—twins, gifted by blood to access the combined power of the Source. In fear for her creations and an echo of the past, Asha and Aniia forged beings of protection and guidance for the Gemini-born blood. **Alexos**.

In admiration and envy of her sister's born blood, stricken with the millstone of destruction, the third sister, Ahnae, pleaded with Asha to aid in giving her a son—a singularity amongst singularities. Through pity and love for her sister, a son was born to the mother of Destruction.

Unruly and just, the son of destruction yearned to be amongst the royals. Through study came unforeseen knowledge. Through knowledge, the unforeseen manifestation of power in the spoken tongue of the texts. Thus, the son was destined to be Charmed—the first **Magi**.

CHAPTER ONE

THE MORNING AIR

The cool morning air seemed to wrap the streets in a dewy mist, hiding those within it from their thoughts and sight—a haven from or a danger to themselves. Chilled enough to have a bite on any bare skin, the crisp air clung to every surface it could touch, streaking down windowpanes, blades of grass, and cars left outside to its will. The occasional glare of passing headlights cut through its thick weight on the world, the refracting illumination flashing before the eyes of Tyler Asoron as he jogged down the quiet road. Tyler had large, bright brown eyes that brought out his sharp facial structure; they sat behind a head of dark hair, which was well-kept.

The air bit his lips as it entered his mouth, numbing his heavy breath and chilling the gathering beads of sweat on his brow. His stride was steady, a typical pace for a morning run before his guardians, Aunt Rebecca and Uncle Rion, awoke.

Tyler never knew his birth parents. He was orphaned before he could remember, his aunt only speaking of how she welcomed the two best decisions she ever made into her life. The first was deciding to raise Tyler after the sudden death of his parents, Aiden and Alina Asoron—a subject she didn't often revisit.

The second was to marry Rion Peters, whom she had met while raising a toddler. Tyler still had the vague memory of their wedding day and eating cake in mind as he picked up pace. The chilling feel of his wet clothes had begun to get to Tyler as he jogged along. To jog in cool weather and be hot or at least warm was one thing, but wet clothes meant the chilled air could bite.

Luckily, he was approaching home. The mist seemed to part for him at his quick pace, eager to reach the finish line. Until finally, he was home. Even though Tyler's momentum ceased, his heart hadn't entirely caught up. His breath was heavy but slowing as he gave in to the cold air, letting it cool and settle him.

The beads of sweat on his brow, now fully realized droplets, trailed down the sides of his face. Tyler moved down the sidewalk slowly toward the front porch and up its steps. As he reached for the keys in his pocket, something strange at his feet caught his eye—a peculiar package. He looked down to see an unmarked box.

A delivery this early?

With curiosity and caution, he bent down to investigate it. The parcel was oblong, black with white ends. Gently lifting it, Tyler felt its unexpected weight. The moment he palmed the box, a sudden crawling cold chill surged through him.

His eyes shot to his surroundings as he stood as if someone were watching him—perhaps a lurking neighbor or wondering passerby, but to his surprise, the air was still. Curious about who would send something so early, Tyler turned the box and searched for a label. To his surprise, once again, on the other side, in very bold lettering, it said *FRAGILE*, with no sender details. Tyler used one of his keys to pierce the taped edge of the box, pulling it open.

Relieved and surprised to see inside was a slender bottle of wine. It had a script on the label, hand-painted, indecipherable, and intriguing. He traced over the unknown words and symbols. There was no note or any indication of who might have sent it.

As Tyler held the bottle, he got an odd feeling that crept over him, a sense of connection to a distant place or time, which gave him a slightly eerie sense. This was a personal delivery. It was then that Tyler recalled the flash of headlights during his run. The lights must have belonged to a delivery truck, though the fog was too thick to be sure. Putting the box beneath his arm, hugged against his ribs, he fumbled with the keys momentarily before reaching for the doorknob.

Just as he did, its locks clicked, and the door swung open. Standing behind it was his aunt Rebecca, wide-eyed. She seemed to be just as surprised to see Tyler as he was her. They stared at each other momentarily, Rebecca brushing her fingers through her tousled brunette locks. "Tyler." She said with a tired voice, stepping aside. Tyler stepped inside, stuffing his keys back into his pocket.

"Morning, Rebecca."

Rebecca wiped her eyes, smiling. She looked more tired than usual, her eyes carrying the weight of the night beneath them and her skin devoid of hydration.

"How was your run, honey?"

"It was—good."

Tyler replied with a worried gaze, holding the box out. Rebecca's eyes fell on it, slowly taking the parcel in hand. "Oh, it finally came. Thank you, Ty." She jingled the box slightly beside her head as if she'd just won a prize.

"Where's the bottle from this time?"

Rebecca sighed, furrowing her brow sharply as she turned the black box. "Spain, I think?"

Tyler's eyes widened. "Cool, could I try some?" Rebecca popped her tongue, cocked her head with sharp eyes. "Kidding, kidding. I'm going to go shower and get ready. Maybe you can get back to sleep before Uncle Rion wakes up," he said, slowly backing away from her in surrender.

He glanced over to the wall of wine bottles, a collection his aunt and uncle had grown over the years. Most were empty or nearly empty. *Fine reds and smooth whites*, they tell him. There were a few other bottles that Tyler wasn't too sure about, all from different sides of the world.

"Does Spain have anything to do with my parents?"

The words hung in the air for an eternity.

"No. They—never had a chance to go." Rebecca's voice was low, almost a whisper. The weight of her sadness was barely concealed just beneath the surface. Her vulnerability was clear to Tyler. He wished he could take back the question.

It was too early in the day or too bold of a question, but Tyler promised himself he'd say what was on his mind and ask the difficult questions to get the truth. He wasn't a kid anymore. Before he could say he was sorry, Rebecca closed the front door. She had her head down when he got to the wine wall. Tyler drew in a deep breath and steadied himself on the staircase. His words hovered on the brink of being spoken before they dissolved into the exhalation of a silent sigh as he watched his aunt.

He swallowed the hard lump, not asking his questions that retreated into the shadows of his mind, choosing, instead, the safety of the unspoken over the risk of disturbing the balance—*not yet.*

"Hope you can even find a spot for it."

He said as he darted up the staircase.

By the time Tyler reached the bottom of the stairs again, it was apparent that the still morning was no longer. Everything and everybody had risen, other than the sun, that is. It hadn't made an appearance in nearly two months. The light was diffused, muted by the threatening gray clouds, the culprits behind the misty mornings. It was dim enough, with the amount of sunlight that streamed through the window shades, to fill the space as best it could—lighting sufficiently to signal the beginning of the morning. "Tyler, hurry, or you'll be late meeting Kyle."

Rebecca said, coming from the kitchen with new vivacity. Her smile was wide, and her brunette locks held back with a clip. She carried a plate of strongly smelling food, which she set down before Tyler as she sat beside him. Tyler crammed the sweater over his shoulder into his school bag before tossing it beside his seat at the table. After all Tyler's years with his aunt and uncle, the morning ritual had stayed pretty much the same: breakfast, small talk, and drives to school. He often reflected on what life would have been like if his parents had been alive.

Tyler plopped himself into the chair at the dining table, wasting no time beginning to stuff his face when he saw Rebecca's world-famous scrambled eggs and bacon. His uncle Rion was at the far end of the table, his face hidden behind an open newspaper. "Slow down there, Ty. I'm sure Kyle will wait for you." He peeked out from behind the pages. "Have you given any more thought to that internship we discussed?"

It was a lifetime opportunity for some: his uncle offered him a summer internship at the medical company he worked for. Tyler paused mid-bite; he had thought it over but hadn't decided. Rion ran the company as the Life Flight Director and head pilot. Tyler had gone with him a couple of times over the years and enjoyed it; however, he wasn't sure that would be a job he would like to do.

In fact, he wasn't sure he wanted a job at all. For as long as he could remember, Tyler had an unquenchable thirst for the world beyond his hometown's familiar borders. Before him was the path of a regular career laid out like a map, which everyone else appeared enthusiastic for him to follow. It felt suffocating. The thought of studying abroad, of the unknown, excited him. The call of wanderlust and learning under foreign skies was all-alluring.

With graduation looming, the pressure was on to decide. Tyler stared at his uncle, mouth full of eggs, swallowing the bite before answering, "I'll think about it some more today." Rion slowly nodded and returned to the newspaper. Before the anxiety could mount as Tyler's mind escaped to the land of expectations, a bolded story on the front page of the paper his uncle held up caught his attention.

ANIMALS FOUND DEAD.

"What's the story on the dead animals?"

Rion flipped the newspaper in half. "Something about a few dead animals in the woods. Probably a bear that didn't quite make it to hibernation yet."

Tyler nodded slightly. It was possible, but for something like that to make the front page or even happen in their town was unusual. Before Tyler could ask for more details, he suddenly felt firm palms squeezing his shoulders.

"There's no rush to decide on your future. You have plenty of time," Rebecca said, smiling. Are you and Kyle getting excited about graduation?"

It was just what Tyler needed to hear; he wiped his mouth, nodding and smiling at her. "We're both excited. Kyle is even giving a speech."

"Well then, should be quite the speech, I'm sure. Are you helping him write it?"

Tyler continued nodding as he stood from the table, pushing away the empty plate.

"Come on, I'll take you to school," Rebecca added.

"And speaking of life decisions, it's about time I got a car. Don't you agree?" Rebecca and Rion burst into short but piercing laughter just before Tyler could finish his sentence.

A likely reaction.

This was not the first time that Tyler had brought it up. He could remember many conversations; his well-seasoned arguments about freedom, responsibility, and convenience were always met with the same chuckles. Each laugh seemed like a gentle pat on the head, a nonverbal *no, not yet, too dangerous*. Since getting his license, Tyler has tried to convince his aunt and uncle that, like most other teens at school, he was ready to drive a car. "Hey, I'm serious this time. I'll be graduating soon. It's time."

"We'll discuss it." Rebecca headed for the front door. "Rion, don't forget to chill the new bottle of wine today. We've been expecting this one for a while." By the time Rebecca pulled into the school parking lot, Tyler's mind hadn't entirely left the awkward interaction earlier in the morning, unsure if it warranted an apology.

"Got everything you need?"

Rebecca asked, pulling Tyler from his thoughts. "Don't worry, I've got everything." He replied, closing the car door behind him. "I love you. Promise we'll discuss the car thing? I don't think you and Rion will want to drive me around my entire life. Besides, I can help pay for it. Maybe get a summer job?"

Rebecca let down the window, smiling, and nodded.

"Yes, I promise. We'll discuss it. Get going, I'm sure Kyle is waiting." Tyler smiled back, sprinting towards the school football field. As he approached the bleachers, he was relieved to see Kyle still patiently waiting for him, tossing a football as he did.

"You're late again," he said as Tyler climbed over a few rows of seats and sat beside him.

"Sorry man, weird morning. How was practice?"

"Well, I finally showed the coach my perfect throw. The other guys weren't impressed."

"Perfect throw, eh?"

Kyle nodded. "Yeah, when the velocity and trajectory are just right, I can—"

Tyler shook his head.

"Too smart for your own good."

"I can't help it. If the coach and the others just listened…"

Tyler laughed; he admired Kyle's ambition, always striving to do better and make improvements. "I get it. You're right, man."

"Anyway, Ty, what's up with you? Still having those wild dreams?" Tyler looked down. How could he forget what has kept him awake most of the night over the past two months? He was swept into the same vivid dream night after night: sky-high above the ground, with the freedom of a bird flying on its own, floating through the expanse of the boundless sky. The world below blanketed by puffs of clouds. An island on the horizon in the distance, opening to blue water below, captivating in isolated beauty.

A sudden shift seemed to derail the flight, turning to despair as if his wings were clipped, sending him on a crash-course plunge toward the open water. Each time, waking just before impact, his heart racing, the lingering echo still present.

"I'm still not sure what they mean."

Tyler looked out into the distance as he recalled the scenes, the tangible weight of his subconscious lingering in the shadows of his mind. "That wasn't even the strangest thing that's happened today."

Kyle shook his head in silence, no longer tossing the football. "What happened?"

"You've seen the wall of wine. Well, when I got back from my run this morning, there was a new bottle at the front door…" Kyle started tossing the football again.

"Okay? That's not very strange."

"Just wait. The box was unmarked, so I opened it. When I did, I got a weird feeling."

Kyle's interest was piqued again as he stopped tossing. "Weird feeling?"

"I don't know how to explain it. Just weird. When I gave the box to Rebecca, she said it was from Spain. So, I asked if Spain had anything to do with my parents."

Kyle shook his head.

"Ty, you know how she gets when it comes to them." Tyler knew he was right. He did know. "It just came out. She didn't say much, just that they never got the chance to visit." Tyler sat back, letting out a sigh. "I just want to know the truth."

"I get it, and I'm sorry Ty," Kyle replied, stuffing the

football into his bag before standing. "We better get going, or we'll be late."

*

The bell sounded for the day as Tyler and Kyle entered the main hall. "I'll catch up with you later!" Kyle shouted, jogging down the hall. Tyler turned down the hive of activity within the school's halls and darted past peers who crossed in front of him. That was one thing Tyler wouldn't miss about high school: all the organized chaos.

One of the perks of being a senior this year was that he didn't have to have a full schedule every day, so instead of rushing to find his first class, Tyler headed to the study hall. No class didn't mean he couldn't study, and more importantly, there were computers in the study hall. Tyler had a sneaking suspicion that there was more to the dead animals found in the woods that he wasn't quite ready to let go of.

As he entered the space, he saw an open chair at a computer and sat down as quickly as he had come in. "And just like that, you're going to walk past and not say hello?"

A familiar voice said from behind. Tyler spun to see the school's librarian and hall supervisor. "Oh, sorry, Ms. Frankel. I just needed to do some research."

"Of course you did. No Kyle today?"

"Nope, just me." He and Kyle frequented the study area, making it a regular hangout whenever they could. Tyler and Kyle were familiar, friendly faces, but that was all changing now that they were graduating.

"Okay. Well, I hope to see you both here soon, at least before graduation." Tyler smiled as Ms. Frankel continued with a stack of books onto her desk. Turning back to the computer screen, he caught a glimpse of a nearby student standing at a bookcase. The student looked a few years older than Tyler.

In any case, he seemed to be too old for a high school library. He was taller than Tyler, with short dark hair, almond skin, and strikingly deep brown eyes. Their eyes met momentarily, and Tyler saw a small smile form at the corner of the boy's mouth. He replied with a slight nod and returned to the screen. It didn't take long to find the headline after a quick search.

ANIMALS FOUND DEAD.

Tyler began reading the article. *Olympus Cove wildlife officials said a hiker wandered out of the woods to find help after finding carcasses on Olympus Trail.*

The trail wasn't far from town. Tyler was familiar with it—North of the new housing development. *A group of friends set out on an early morning hike to Oly Falls, the Chief of the Wildlife Department said in a news release. Wildlife officials said they lost their way during the trek, forcing the group to spend the night in the cold woods.*

The next day, one group member wandered outside of camp, discovering the trail and the dead animals with it. Panicked, the man then found his way out of the woods without his friends to help, officials said. Rescuers began searching the area and discovered over a dozen animal carcasses in the woods, seemingly drained of their blood. Wildlife officials said the animals were "fatally injured." According to reports, the attack was most likely a larger predator.

The area is currently under further investigation. Caution is in place for locals on hiking trails as the whereabouts of the predatory animal are still unknown, and it is presumed to be a danger to people.

Drained of blood? The words lingered in Tyler's head. What kind of predator would drain blood from an animal? Tyler suddenly felt a presence behind him as he continued questioning his thoughts.

Another crawling cold chill surged through him.

His head spun to where he had seen the person at the bookshelves before and then to the front desk where Ms. Frankel sat, but no one was around. Tyler cautiously returned to the screen. At the bottom of the article was an email and phone number for questions. Tyler quickly noted the details on his phone and logged out of the computer. He needed to talk to Kyle.

CHAPTER TWO

THE ILLUSIONISTS

A sense of electricity seemed to fill the late afternoon air as cheers sounded throughout the packed stadium for yet another touchdown. Every play warranted excitement from the fans. You could feel it within the air—as if energy crackled along everyone's skin. The bleachers were a complete sea of green and gold colors under the darkening grey sky. The stadium lights lit up the field like a stage set for a play.

The cool air was filled with chatter as Tyler watched with pride—Kyle Huntington leading his team to another incoming victory. He made some of what Tyler assumed had to be the perfect throw he had just mentioned, but school was a distant blur now. After Tyler had taken his seat in his first class, time had sped up. One class period wove into the other in a continuous ribbon. The lectures became a muffled hum to his ears, like background noise from a fan that increased over the day.

Tyler's mind was elsewhere, whirling with thoughts on the article and the animals drained of blood. The article didn't say what they found at the sight. He wondered if there were any predator prints or footprints. And since the animals were bloodless, what about bite marks? Tyler needed Kyle's scientific brain to figure it out. Watching the game after classes was nice, but he needed to pick his friend's brain afterward.

As the game went on, Tyler began to feel a shift in the air, first, with the few drops of rain—a subtle patter atop the play's background—developing into a drizzle and, at last, into a general downpour, sparkling like snowflakes as they fell beneath the lights. Neither set of fans relented. Ponchos and umbrellas popped out across the field among the opposing team's fans, who were indifferent to the whole affair. Some other students passed them around from one of the game attendants, and Tyler got his raincoat from the pile. The cheers returned, going up to a new level when the noise of the deluge became piercing.

Tyler looked over the crowd before him and was impressed with the resilience of so many people, yet he got tripped up by the sight of one attendee—an anomaly. Uncovered, unprotected, and allowing the rain to do its bidding. The color in their face was washed out, emotionless—and familiar.

As Tyler looked closer, he recognized the student from the library—the one from the bookcase. But his dark hair changed, drenched, big curls dripping and sticking to his pale-toned face. His eyes were fixed as if glossed over on something ahead of him—the deep brown eyes Tyler remembered now golden-hued embers in the distance. Again, he felt that sudden crawl of cold chill now that their eyes met.

Tyler squinted as he could hardly see through the unrelenting rain; he was questioning himself. Were they really that golden? What attracted his eyes to him? Who was this?

Tyler broke away, eyes dropping momentarily, the rain a curtain of distortion. Pulling his droplet-stained glasses from his face, he found a small dry area of fabric under the poncho and cleaned them. Returning to the figure with clearer sight, but it was gone. Had he imagined it? There was doubt mixed at the forefront of his mind, the distinctive image of those glowing eyes etched into his thoughts.

The final blow of the whistle brought Tyler back from the maelstrom. It had sealed the victory for the home team with an uproar from the stands. Tyler watched as Kyle celebrated with his teammates on the muddied field terrain before they exited. As the crowd filtered out, Tyler went along with the traffic outside the stadium, looking forward to catching up with Kyle as the game ended.

Tyler stood at the stadium's gates in front of the parking lot. The mad surge of people quickly dwindled into a hush. Tyler walked one way and then turned around to look for Kyle. When he heard a commotion behind the stadium doors, his steps stopped.

He looked through the bars of the gates at the bleachers where a group of students stood in opponents' school colors and branded jackets. Cornering someone Tyler couldn't quite make out, taunts being shouted—an ugly scene. Tyler hurried inside, met instantly by a younger student who was breaking out of the group and coming towards him.

"Are you okay?" His face was filled with fear, and he nodded. Tyler helped him out of the gate, bag in hand, clutching a backpack and books close to his chest, then Tyler turned back to the group of students. "What's your problem?" Tyler barked, voice steady and insistent. His intervention was audacious and possibly reckless, with him outnumbered the way he was, but standing by was not an option for him—not while someone was in need. One student, a solid-built male with a menacing face, snorted and spat on the metal bleachers—the clear leader of the pack.

"That game was rigged." He gritted through his teeth as he and the others descended.

"Looked to be a fair win from where I was sitting." Tyler shot back. The pack was within just a few feet. The rest were roughly Tyler's height, but their ringleader had no claim on additional vertical inches. His eyes were frosty, and there was a snarl on his wet face from the deluge or his own physical exertion. He gazed, sucking on a toothpick at the corner of his lips, the sprinkle of the rain continuing.

"Do we have a problem here?" The leader asked.

Tyler remained silent but composed in front of the group. He looked down at them with toughened eyes, hiding any feeling of intimidation to the depths of his being. "No problem here as long as you keep to yourselves." Tyler was shocked by the roughness of his voice; it was a tone all unfamiliar to him.

"Is that so? And if we don't?" The boy replied with a chuckle, smiling to the left and right of him. One of the others was cracking their knuckles as if preparing to use them in a fist, but his threats were weightless. Tyler was not one for physical violence, but he would defend himself and others if necessary.

"I think it's about time you all cleared out of here." A voice came from behind the group.

Tyler looked past them to see Kyle standing a few feet away. The leader of the pack spun to meet Kyle's gaze. "What was that?" He spat again. Kyle's eyes flicked to Tyler, then locked with the boy. The others surrounded Kyle as a creeping light fog rolled over the field, adding an aura to the already-charged atmosphere. Kyle stood as defiantly as Tyler did, with his backpack slung over his shoulder and his football helmet in hand. The tension was rising, and as it did, another distant voice sliced through the standoff.

"Trouble, trouble..."

It was a voice that seemed to come from nowhere and everywhere. Through the misty cloud, Tyler spotted unmistakably the pair of golden eyes flash again, even from this distance. But now, the form was not alone; another came and equally matched its presence. The tension shattered at the sight and sound of the voice, and the angry group whirled about in circles, first trying to find the source of the voice before focusing on the figures.

In a state of fear and confusion, the other followers of the pack leader scattered in all directions, leaving the leader alone on the field. "Who's...who's there? What is that?" he blubbered, sliding in the wet grass and landing on his rear end. He thrashed around in a puddle for a moment before climbing back up to his feet, pushing Tyler out of the way as he ran towards the gate. Tyler was just about ready to decide that he should run as well when the creeping cold chill passed through him again. Kyle stayed put, staring at where the figures had been.

"Ky? Maybe we should go too."

Kyle gave no response. Tyler approached him, tapping his arm. "Let's get out of here. You're my ride, remember?" Kyle turned to meet Tyler's eyes for a moment. When they turned back the figures were no more.

"Who are they?" Kyle said, an eerie calm in his voice.

Tyler shook his head.

"New students? Rivals? I have no idea. I thought I saw one of them in the library before." A weird presence loomed over the field as Tyler and Kyle left the stadium. Tyler felt a strange sense of clarity come over him now, this particular feeling that the figures were not just figments of his imagination but real, tangible beings—and now, he wasn't the only one who saw them.

*

It was a ride with no words, only the soft echo of the radio and the running engine to fill the silence in the air—for the most part, that is. Outside Tyler's window, the world formed into blurs of shadows and lights, moving past quickly as though corresponding to his own somewhat chaotic thoughts. Tyler retold the strange encounter with the bullies and the reappearance of the figure—or figures. "What happened back there?" Kyle asked.

"I was waiting for you outside the stadium when I heard them messing with someone. I had to say something when I saw them towering over a younger kid."

Kyle reached for the radio knob, turning it off.

"Of course you did, I would've too—but it was four against one. Did they hurt anyone?"

Tyler shook his head. "I don't think so. The kid broke away and ran off. That's when they turned on me." Tyler glanced over at Kyle, noticing the contemplative expression shadowing his face. As if his thoughts were miles away, lost in a sea of reflection. Tyler could tell something bothered him about it all. "Ky, what is it?"

There was another short silence before Kyle answered, his eyes focused on the road ahead, perhaps working through a mental puzzle. "I'm glad no one was hurt. I, I just keep picturing those figures…that voice."

Tyler leaned forward.

"Did you recognize them?"

"I'm not sure. Couldn't place it. Just a feeling I got."

"I got a weird feeling seeing them, too," Tyler replied. The confessions seemed to hang between them, a new unresolved mystery. "Speaking of strange, did you hear about the animals in the woods? The ones drained of blood?"

Kyle glanced from the road to meet Tyler's for a second.

"I heard something about it, more than likely an environmental factor affecting the wildlife—like a disease outbreak or toxicity in the woods," Kyle answered hastily, with an analytical tone. Tyler was taken aback by how quickly he came to such a conclusion. "And come to think of it, the figures and the voice we heard probably also have some logical explanation. Our brains are just wired to find patterns and rationalize things, particularly in stressful situations. It could be just a convenient trick of the mind."

Tyler listened, absorbing the flow of logic. After all, Kyle was a wealth of knowledge. It was a bit of clarity in all the murkiness that the scientific lens provided, unlike the murky waters of his superstitions. However, Tyler could not help but feel more of the mystery gnawing at him, unable to settle with the beacon of reason in this fog of uncertainty. The night's shadows seemed to be slowly creeping into the reality of their small town.

He was almost certain he had seen the same person in the school library at the bookcase earlier that day. Didn't he? And now others had seen the figures, too. "Sure. That makes sense, but we all saw the same thing simultaneously."

"Convenient trick of the mind—a collective experience," Kyle added. Tyler stood at the crossroads between science and fiction, only half able to let himself believe it was real because of the reason Kyle presented.

He went into his phone from the depths of his front

pant pocket. "There was a contact number for questions and tips on the article," he said aloud, his voice steady against the car's quiet. "I should contact that reporter who ran this." Kyle looked at him again, a flicker of reluctance dancing in his eyes as the car pulled up the driveway to Tyler's home. The humming engine was about to wind down to its comforting purr, signaling the end of their ride, if not their quest for answers.

"Yeah. There's no harm in asking," Kyle answered, his voice sympathetic. There was more to it, something Tyler had missed. A depth that he heard beckoning him with some siren song of secrets. Tyler grabbed his bag and opened the door, leaning down to the open window with a sincere smile of thanks, meeting Kyle's eyes.

"Thanks for the ride home," he said. "And Ky, your dad would have been proud to see you win the game tonight. Great job." Time seemed to hold its breath suddenly as Tyler watched his words settle in on Kyle. Even in the fortress of strength and knowledge that he was, Tyler knew how he felt about his late father. His mouth opened to say something—anything—to weave words of gratitude, but instead, they stayed prisoners locked inside the confines of his lips. Tyler saw sadness flicker across his face, a mere tilting of his expression that painted a picture of a thousand lifetimes of sorrow. Finally, Kyle nodded slowly, and Tyler mirrored the movement—their shared acknowledgment of the bittersweet moment. This nod carried so much weight of gratitude, grief, and deep understanding.

"Thank you," Kyle finally said, his voice soft.

CHAPTER THREE

THE REDS & WHITES

Pushing open the front door, Tyler was instantly surrounded by heat as he stepped inside, vividly contrasting with the cold, dewy night air. He followed the faint clinking of glassware and murmurs toward the dining room. Seated there, his aunt and uncle sat under the soft glow of the chandelier light, their quiet dialogue trailing off as he entered. "Tyler, you're home just in time for dinner. How was the game?" His aunt Rebecca asked, holding a glass.

The dining table was set with three steaming plates of food at each setting. It was another pot roast and potatoes night, one of Rebecca's specialties. However, when she loves something, the household loves it for weeks. "It was good. Kyle led his team to yet another victory."

His uncle Rion chuckled, "Of course he did."

Rebecca sat back in her chair, an arm across her chest, as she brought the glass of deep red liquid to her lips. It was a rich crimson red, darker than previous bottles Tyler had seen. He noted how the light danced through it, casting a ruby reflection on the table below.

"Yeah, it was a good game." Throwing his bag beside him, Tyler dropped into the chair opposite it. His uncle Rion was nearly done with his plate of food, leaning back with a book. A picture of contentment, yet curiously without a glass of his own. And it struck Tyler then—despite the countless foreign bottles that lined the infamous wall, he had never seen his uncle partake in any of them. Tyler thought on this as he looked over the plate before him.

Of course, his uncle did not leave Rebecca to drink by herself; there was no way she could have drunk all those bottles herself. It wasn't until the first fork full of roast that the peculiarity was dismissed from his mind. After another two, the thought was just another quirk of his uncle Rion's personal taste.

"It must have been a long day," Rebecca remarked, her voice smooth with an underlying thread of curiosity. Tyler just nodded and breathed out, sitting back from his plate. Her words pulled a thread of memory. The evening's events returned in flashes, and with them, the mysteries lingered. Tyler considered mentioning the strange figures and the run-in with the bullies for a moment, but he wasn't sure there was much to tell.

"It was. Classes were long, and I ended up doing some research on those dead animals in the woods." He replied.

Rebecca took another sip from her glass. "I see. Find anything interesting?"

"An article—about what happened. It said they were—" Tyler trailed off as he watched Rebecca turn the glass up until it was emptied. He had thought her almost eager enough to lick up the last trickle, and that seemed to be the only thing she held back because of his and Uncle Rion's presence. She seemed to draw it out, eyes closing momentarily after she had finished, and the empty glass was back on the table. "Is that from the bottle that arrived this morning? Is it everything you expected?" Tyler's voice carried a few undertones of concern. The curiosity that had dwindled from his mind suddenly rekindled when he thought about his aunt drinking all those bottles alone.

"Exquisite." She replied, meeting Tyler's gaze.

"Yes, truly one of the finest we've had, I'd say."

Rion added.

Tyler turned to his uncle, "You tried some uncle?"

He nodded. "Of course, I had a glass earlier."

His uncle's smooth words quickly dismissed any lingering concern, but Tyler could not shake the feeling that perhaps his uncle sensed his hesitation and was only trying to appease him. He decided to leave the topic as is for the time being. "I'm glad you both enjoy it," he replied with a polite smile. As Tyler settled himself into his chair, his eyes flicked back over the now empty glass, the remnants of deep red coating the inside.

The time seemed fitting for a second chance, a conversation; the liquid would provide the space to pose the long-over-due question in his mind. "Rebecca, when you said my parents didn't have the chance to visit Spain…"

Tyler started.

His voice was steady, but his words hung delicately in the air. His aunt and uncle's silent reactions were telling. The pause was like a door left ajar, open to the past, waiting for Tyler to enter. "Aiden and Alina didn't have the chance to do many things."

Rebecca's reply was dry, soiled by the red liquid. She hesitated for a second, her eyes now on the empty glass as if she was drawing strength from what had been inside it. "They were remarkable people, full of life, dreams, and adventure." Rebecca reached for the matte black bottle within reach and began pouring into the glass; the red liquid reflected a world of untold stories back at Tyler as it gurgled and rippled, finding stillness with a delicate dance of bubbles at its surface. "Honestly, I think of them every time we a drink like this. They believed in savoring every moment, finding wonder in the smallest things."

Her words were surprising and welcome to Tyler's ears, painting a picture of his parents he'd never seen before—adventurers, dreamers, seekers of more beyond the surface. Something he resonated with deeply. That felt very relatable deep down. Rebecca's vagueness was deliberate; it just deepened Tyler's thoughts about his parents that much more. It was hazy, but Tyler could see one thing: Aiden and Alina Asoron had lived as complete a life as the red substance in Rebecca's hand.

The air was charged with the vibrations of yesteryears and the never-to-have-beens, binding Tyler to what he had not lived through. An oppressive silence hung over the table. He looked down at his emptied plate, then at the others on the table, the remains of their meal that supported the long-awaited discussion. Rebecca finished the second, possibly third, glass of red liquid.

Placing the once again emptied vessel on the table.

"Let me help clean up tonight." Tyler offered, standing, easing the intensity of the moment, gratitude in his voice for the rarity of the conversation.

"That's very sweet of you," Rebecca replied while Rion nodded in agreement, expressing his appreciation. Tyler smiled and began gathering the dishes.

Cleanup was a slow act that evening as the thoughts of Tyler's parents remained. Dishes clinked in the background as he delved further into his thoughts. His hands worked mechanically at the kitchen sink. Moving together in tandem, one dish after another, into the soapy water. Tyler returned to the dining table to pick up the near-emptied bottle of red liquid and the glass.

As he screwed the lid on, something about the dark, almost menacing liquid inside gnarled at Tyler. He carried the glass back to the sink; the thick residue that had clung within it emitted a pungent, metallic smell starkly reminiscent of blood. Suddenly, a strange realization prickled at the edge of Tyler's consciousness. Not familiar with the smell or taste of a bottled liquid like this, he shrugged off the uneasy feeling. He rinsed it out, and the smell went away. But still, something lingered in the quiet kitchen. More unease, maybe? It was as though the glass had whispered secrets to Tyler, best left unexplored.

Tyler's suspicion was quickly greeted with the return of the crawling shiver, again shaking down his spine. Lifting his eyes from the sink, he was met with a pang in his chest at the sight of the window before him. The window held a shadow, a jagged, ghostly, near-transparent figure with a pair of the same glowing golden eyes piercing through the glass. Then suddenly, it was gone as fast as it had come, the sight of the ghostly presence leaving Tyler with a tremble in his hands as they moved faster, his vision locked to the still quiet night beyond the window. Soon, the bottle and dishes were swiftly tucked away.

Tyler's mind raced with more questions.

Had he seen what he thought he had? Did the figures from the game now follow him home? Questions were flitting through his mind like leaves in the wind. One question stayed prominent: Could the shadowed figures have something to do with the chilling article on the animals in the woods? Now, the haunting eyes of gold returned to his mind and burned themselves into his memory: an image as haunting as it was mesmerizing now that he lay in bed.

Retreating to the perceived safety of the room, he lay completely still in darkness with his eyes wide open, heart pounding steadily in his chest. The night grew long, with Tyler tossing and turning, looking for that elusive sleep comfort for hours. His every tick on the clock reminded him to question everything beyond his understanding: his late parents, the shadowed figures, and most of all, his guardians.

CHAPTER FOUR

THE SLEEPLESS NIGHT

Time was an illusion, a thread in a woven sweater of days, hours, and weeks. Each is a subtle imprint on Tyler and the world. For him, the days slipped by all too quickly while the nights he spent awake had stuck to his mind with rather unsettling clarity. At times, Tyler caught himself in the grips of the dream and its vivid imagery—a night spun from shadows. A twisted mirror of his reality, where darkness reigned—haunted by the piercing glow of golden eyes. Surely the same eyes belonging to the one from the library bookcase—and football field, wasn't it? Tyler still couldn't decide.

The replay pulled him back to that sleepless night, and

Tyler again saw this influential figure from his dreamscape in his head, its movements unnaturally fast, a blur. And the high-pitched scream that had suddenly split the air was the unmistakable sound of a dying animal. Part of Tyler wanted to race to the defense of the thing he could only hear, while another part just screamed at him to run away from the nightmare. Before either could happen, the earth beneath him collapsed, sending Tyler into a river of liquid so thick and red. It was blood, lukewarm and suffocating, covering him in its iron-scented embrace—the same aromatic scent that came from the residue on the glass.

Tyler fought for breath within the dream, every stroke of his arms an utterance for escape from the tide that was the rivers until finally, he awoke with a start, heart jumping and skin clammy with sweat, to the unending buzz of his phone being the savor of nightmares that brought him back to waking reality. This dream was so vivid and frightening, unlike any other night terrors he had ever experienced. It stayed in his mind: a clarity transcended any other dream.

"Tyler, where did you drift off to this time?" Rebecca's

voice cut through the imagery like a sharp blade.

"Sorry, what were you saying?" Tyler sat in the car's front seat, drifting back to reality from the sea of thoughts, soothed by the road's quiet.

"You've been miles away these past few weeks. Something on your mind?" Rebecca asked, her voice gentle with reproach. Tyler felt guilty, aware of the recent preoccupation with his thoughts, but shook his head anyway. Then, the conversation took an unexpected turn when Tyler heard Rebecca ask him a question about cars.

"So, what did you think your first car might be?" Her words landed with the surprise of a thunderclap. Tyler was completely caught off guard, struggling to form a response, scrambling to process the sudden shift in conversation.

"No rush, give it some thought. Maybe we can go look at cars this weekend," she added, her eyes softening as she observed Tyler's struggle. She paused. Tyler watched the thoughtful expression on her face as she looked to the road. "There is something else I wanted to mention, too," she began, her voice taking on a more serious tone. "About your parents…" She hesitated as if weighing her words carefully. It had been a few weeks since pot roast and potato night, and the subject of Tyler's parents hadn't come up again.

"There may be some old friends of theirs that might come into town soon. Friends you won't remember, but they knew you when you were just a baby." The idea sparked a flicker of curiosity in Tyler, but before he could find the words, the car stopped before his high school. Rebecca's words lingered with him for a moment longer.

"What do you think?"

"I guess I'm just surprised. We've never talked about my parents this much before, but I'm glad we are. But Rebecca, why now? Who are these friends?"

Tyler met Rebecca's gaze again.

"It's about time we did. We'll talk more when you get home. Don't be late, get going."

*

School was the last thing weighing on Tyler's mind today; the morning's revelations and the nightmare from weeks ago were bearing down. The high school hallways buzzed with familiar chaos of students chattering and locker slams just as the final bell sounded. As the school day unfolded, Tyler was in history class, half-listening to the lecture. Mr. Witwer's words flowed over him, a river of dates and events until a particular topic snagged his attention.

"Creatures of the night," the teacher announced, "a part of folklore for centuries." Images of dark, mythical creatures flashed on the screen at the front of the class—a cascade into modern-day predators. Tyler's thoughts immediately raced back to the golden glowing eyes.

"As some may have heard, several dead animals were recently discovered on the Oly Trail. Who knows what type of creature of the night might have done this?" At first, the classroom was silent, as if the mention of the creatures had conjured an atmosphere of disbelief. The silence was palpable as slowly the room began to stir with possible speculation. Whispers fluttered like nocturnal wings as theories were debated.

"Wolves?" One student called out.

"Or something worse." Another added.

"A serial killer!" Someone shouted.

Tyler sat in the cauldron of theories and conjectures, his mind racing. The question was more than academic for him. The discussions reflected his internal debates, the same debates in his head since the sighting of the shadowed figures on the football field, now at the top of his mind.

As time passed, the clock's hands inched closer to the hour, and the classroom's energy reached a new height, a symphony of ideas and possibilities. Mr. Witwer stood at the front of the class, observing the fervor. "Excellent class. These are the kinds of considerations you should be making. Nothing is outside the realm of possibility." Just then, the suddenness of the school bell sounded, slicing through the animated chatter.

Books were closed with a soft thud, chairs scraped against the floor, and the room gradually emptied, leaving Tyler alone with the echoes of the lingering discussion. He gathered his things, heading for the classroom door before turning back to Mr. Witwer.

"Do you believe that?" He asked, "That nothing is outside the realm of possibility?" Tyler turned and met the gaze of his teacher. His expression steady as he cleared his throat.

"I do." He started, "If history has taught us anything, the world holds many mysteries."

Tyler nodded slowly, Mr. Witwer's words resonating deeply with him. The ringing of the second bell was a reminder of the line between the world of the unknown and the reality waiting for Tyler outside the classroom.

*

By the end of the day, Tyler found himself in the library again. The hours blurred into a swift current that carried him through the remainder of his classes. Despite the rush of time, his mind remained anchored to the question of creatures of the night. He sat at the computer screen again, this time checking for a response from the reporter he reached out to a few weeks ago. But to his expected surprise, there was no response to his inquiry.

Tyler decided to take his research to the digital archives

on the web. He scanned through the virtual library, finding pieces of information like a puzzle of an ever-growing picture. His focus narrowed on creatures that drained their prey of blood—the mythical vampires. The eerie details of the tales and myths added to the growing connection to the shadowy figure from his nightmare.

Nothing is outside of the realm of possibility.

The words rang in his head again as his search continued. Among the legends was an obscure reference to a story about the existence of modern-day beings who chose to consume life essence in a strange form of aerated blood.

*…it is believed by some that bloodsuckers still exist among us today. Preying on the blood and disguising it in the form of beverages…the beverage of the night creatures…*the grotesque and fascinating story held Tyler in a tight grip. Beverages? His senses were instantly filled with the pungent memory of the metallic smell in Rebecca's glass, the deep red liquid.

Impossible.

His imagination fired at the possibility the thought suggested. A sudden rush of memories flooding his mind: seeing a tired and weary aunt one day and a vibrant and lively being the next night. The many deliveries of exotic bottled beverages. Was it truly possible? No. Tyler needed more concrete evidence and understanding.

He continued to read the source, searching for its author…*no one knows the source of the midnight beverages, but it will be uncovered soon*…the end of the page was signed with only the name Phoenix and dated nearly seven years ago. A quick cross-reference of the pen name uncovered a collection of more posts from the mysterious storyteller.

A cascade of tales and legends about creatures, beings outside the realm of belief: the writings were more than academic; these were personal. Much like Tyler, this was a seeker of truths hidden in the shadows. The articles led to one final post, the last marked differently than the others. An end to the saga…*there isn't much time left for me here*…the author painfully revealed an unknown illness that would eventually claim their life.

The words puddled in Tyler's mind, dreadful to read.

Within the words of Phoenix was still some light of

hope, a farewell with a subtle undercurrent of something more—a return of some kind—another life, another piece of the puzzle.

Lost in his research, Tyler only noticed that time had passed when Kyle appeared beside him suddenly. His presence pulled him back from the chasm of questioning. "Do you believe in creatures of the night?" Tyler asked, his voice steeped in skepticism and curiosity, but his eyes unmoved from the screen. "More specifically, creatures who drain their prey of blood." He added, turning to Kyle. His face showed how caught off guard he was by the question. The weighing of his response in his eyes as Kyle's face softened.

"It's hard to say what's out there," he replied with an uncertain tone. "Science gives us all logic and reason of nocturnal creatures. I'm sure there is more to be explored and discovered."

"There must be more. With all the strange events in town recently, and now, these writings from this person, Phoenix—"

"Phoenix?" Kyle interjected, "Ty, there is all kinds of

misinformation out there."

"Not this. They were just as curious as I am. They knew something." There was silence, and Kyle must have picked up on Tyler's whirling thoughts on the topic, changing the subject.

"We should go. I need to be home after I drop you off." This broke Tyler's concentration, settling him back to reality. He nodded, gathering his things, as he returned to normalcy, however brief it might be this time. The weight of the newly discovered information drew more questions than answers, lingering with Tyler as a silent companion as he and Kyle stepped into the fading light of the day.

PART II

CHAPTER FIVE

ENTER FAMILY FRIENDS

On every turn that car took into Tyler's neighborhood, the houses and trees helped him feel back at home. The trip was not very long, but it was quiet. Free of the constant turbulence of thought raging in Tyler's day. They turned onto the street he lived on, and he remembered that conversation with his aunt.

Looking over at Kyle, who was focused on the road, Tyler wasn't sure he could let the spur-of-the-moment talk go. "I almost forgot," he started, "my aunt said something wild this morning." He paused for a second. Kyle was visibly curious and prompted Tyler to continue. "She said that some family friends of my parents, people I wouldn't remember, of course, might be coming to town soon." Kyle was silent at first, an expression of confusion on his face as the car pulled up to Tyler's house. The engine was idling as they sat, and the words hung between them.

"Would they happen to have a car that looks like it was just driven off a new car lot?" He said finally, looking in the rear-view mirror. Tyler's head spun. A black car, slick and shining, was parked across the street behind them: an antidote to the oppressive, cloud-laden evening. As the meager light sparkled off the car's glossy surface like a liquid mirror, the reflections that it sent back seemed almost like some sort of play of gentle radiance. It even appeared as though the curves and outlines of the vehicle were emphasized by that glossy shine, making it seem almost surreal against the dew-filled air. Droplets clung to its surface, enhancing the delicate sheen that emphasized its untouched condition.

"No way." Tyler said, his voice nearly breathless, "She

said sometime soon, not today!" Nerves began to settle in, a tremble in Tyler's breath. What was he supposed to expect?

"Do you want me to go in with you?"

Kyle asked gently.

"No. You can't. You have to get home." Tyler replied as he spun back in his seat, his gaze low, "I just can't believe they're here. It has to be them, right?"

Kyle nodded.

"I would be surprised if it weren't," he replied hesitantly, "I'm sure it won't be as bad as you think." Tyler's heart was in his throat, but he knew Kyle was right. After all, this was what he wanted and still wanted, right? Taking a deep breath, he opened the car door.

"Thanks, Ky." He said, stepping out of the car with uncertain confidence.

"Just call or text me later?" Kyle added.

Tyler nodded, shutting the door. He decided it would be best to go through the garage entrance, giving himself a few more seconds to brace for impact. Tyler approached the keypad, looking back at Kyle, who gave him a nod of confidence he was still trying to secure within himself. As the car head-lights disappeared, Tyler returned to the keypad, punching in digits and opening the garage.

Every second was a thousand years, each stride to the door another two centuries. Until finally, Tyler's hand was on the doorknob. With a concoction of emotions, he exited, entering the house. As he closed the door behind him, his ears flooded with a symphony of sounds, like waves crashing onto a distant shore.

Distant chatter filled the air, and among the murmurs were clear tones of laughter. The chorus was punctuated by the soft music in the background, wafting down the hall like a breeze. A sharp pang of emotion overwhelmed Tyler for a moment. Rebecca hadn't told him anything about the family. Where had they come from? What were their names? With each stride down the hall came another thought racing into Tyler's mind. It was typical for Rebecca to provide him with such cryptic information; she had a talent for evading tough questions, especially about his parents.

But perhaps that was all beginning to change now.

It was as though the world had stopped by the time Tyler reached the end of the hall. No longer did his feet move; no longer did he breathe. The hall stretched behind him to eternity, and at the brink of it around the corner, was the unknown. It was not only a physical halt but a mental one as well, and the walls seemed to hold their breath as Tyler did. It was as though the hallway were a metaphorical runway, leading him to the very edge of takeoff.

Tyler's senses became magnified within the stillness, keyed in on subtle sounds that quietly enhanced—but nothing remained except for the soft music. The distant chatter was drained as if his known presence was drawing the air out of the room he was about to enter. "Tyler? Come, meet the Scotlers," Rebecca's voice called from around the corner.

With another deep breath, he prepared to round the corner, stepping from the familiar stretch of the hallway into the room of possibilities. Emerging from behind the wall, Tyler was greeted by a quartet of individuals on the couch, each exuding a unique presence. His aunt was seated to their left in an armchair, his uncle resting on its back beside Rebecca in a comforting pose. The sitting figures were the most delicate, alien-like creatures Tyler had ever encountered. They all moved so delicately, slowly, and quickly but deliberately as if they would snap at any minute: a woman, a man, and two others a bit younger than the man.

The man stood, speaking in a low, calm voice.

"Hello, Tyler," he said, extending a hand toward him.

Tyler cleared his throat, clutching his backpack tightly.

"Nice to meet you," he replied, shaking the man's cool, smooth hand like a stone plucked from a cold stream. The man stood out, towering over Tyler, wearing a long coat covering his bulky physique. His short, bright blonde hair was a prominent feature, perfectly styled, each strand meticulously in place. His eyes were striking, catching Tyler's gaze, a vivid blue that could look deep into the soul of any being.

Though the colors were vivid, there was a dullness.

To his left was a woman with an equally striking appearance. Short, curly dark brown hair surrounded the contour of her face, lively with spirals that caught the light in the room and danced on her skin, lush in its honey tones and smooth like a blank canvas. Her eyes were dulled like the man's but deep, dark brown, with a certain depth, like pools of still water under a twilight sky. She smiled with an open expression, catching Tyler's gaze.

"My name is James Scotler," he said, "and this is my family, my wife Diana, and our sons Caleb and Kodi." Tyler managed to smile and nod as James spoke; then, he looked to the rest of the family. The twins—Tyler assumed by the uncanny resemblance—were a couple of years older than him, about 19 or so. They both seemed about the same height as James but shared in their mother's traits otherwise: deep brown eyes, smooth canvas skin, and a head of curls. Their faces flickered a sense of familiarity in Tyler's mind, but he couldn't quite place them. There was such a strong resemblance between the Scotlers and such beauty.

"You look so much like your father," Diana said, still smiling. Her voice carried a strong accent, a blended and shaken French and perhaps German twang. Tyler froze, eyes wide at the sound of it, lingering on every word as if following subtitles to catch every pronunciation.

"Nice to meet you all," he finally replied, breaking his awkward gaze. Tyler looked to his aunt and uncle, who watched intently as if waiting for his reaction. He arched a brow in their direction as if trying to reach for answers in the space above. The look was more than surprise; it was a mixture of hurt and bewilderment, a wordless scream of, *why didn't you tell me?* He attempted another small smile before crossing to the only available chair in front of his guardians, nearest the twins. He flung his bag down by him.

"Apologies for our unexpected arrival," James said.

"No problem, James. I was telling Tyler about you this morning." Rebecca replied. Tyler nearly had the nerve to give a witty remark. Sure, she told me they would visit soon, not the same day. But the urge backed off as the conversation progressed. "Did you enjoy your recent travels?"

Rebecca continued.

"We did. We visited a few distant friends. Our favorite place was Spain, which has the most exquisite architecture. You received the latest bottle we sent to you, yes?"

Tyler's eyes shot up to James.

"You've been sending the bottles?" he blurted out, his finger pointed at the infamous wall behind them. James smiled and nodded, glancing at the wall.

"We have—I suppose—I am the vinitor." Tyler shot another look at Rebecca, then again at James. Rebecca opened her mouth to speak but only let out what would have been words had she decided on the order in which they would come out and stuck to it. Instead, she laughed awkwardly.

"I—we—yes, you are quite the connoisseur James. Tyler, the Scotlers, and I have exchanged several letters and packages. A bit old-fashioned, but it works for us."

The room was silenced again as if the air had been vacuumed up from around them. "We aren't young like you, Tyler," Rion interjected, "we're not used to the WhatsBook or the Face App thingy. Hey, what's that social platform thing the vegans stay away from? MeatUp, or meat something..."

Normally, Tyler would have laughed off one of Uncle Rion's famous failed Dad jokes, but today, it felt like Rion was trying to change the subject away from the packages, leaving Tyler feeling something was still hidden. "How long have you all known each other anyway?" Tyler asked.

The room fell silent again, the words freezing time itself instantly. Heads turned, all attention converging in on Rebecca as the question lingered.

"He should know, Becca," Diana said. Her accent made words melt like butter in a hot pan. The sentence turned ripples with the room. Tyler's eyes twinkled with interest, and he leaned in from his chair, a small glimmer of curiosity illuminated within. He noticed Rion's reaction: brows furrowed, knitted together, an expression of concern or disapproval.

"Diana," Rebecca replied sternly, exchanging a few glances with her before looking up to Rion at her side. Caleb shifted uncomfortably in his seat while Kodi nodded thoughtfully, agreeing with Diana's statement.

"Know what?" Tyler spat out anxiously.

"I was planning on telling you more before their arrival," Rebecca replied softly.

"Things are different now," James said, adding to the ominous atmosphere. Rebecca met Rion's gaze again, this time with a nod. He stood hesitantly, walking over to the infamous wall and pulling an empty bottle, its contents long since enjoyed. He lifted its top in the practiced motion of his hands, and it was more than it appeared. The top gave way from itself, obviously harboring a secret, a cunning disguise of a false top. With both parts in hand, Rion returned to the group and held the bottom half out to Rebecca. She reached in, pulling out a nestled envelope from inside. The eyes in the room now suddenly converged on Tyler as she spoke.

"This was given to us by your parents many years ago."

Tyler's eyes darted over the envelope, a quick flash of knowing—or maybe expecting—swirling in his face. Her hands were steady on the envelope as she stood, crossing the room and holding it out to Tyler. It was smaller than it appeared from a distance. Tyler hesitated when he reached for it. The moment he laid his hand on its surface, the creeping cold chill shot through him. An elaborate wax seal was imprinted on the reverse side of it; the seal carried a symbol of royalty, a large capital letter "V" elaborately intertwined within its emblem, leading him to believe it held something extraordinary. As Tyler weighed the envelope in his hand, which seemed heavier than it should have been, he felt its contents were promising of the truth.

"Can I open it now?"

"Perhaps it's best to wait," James interjected.

"Yes, we will have time to discuss later," Diana added. Rebecca returned to her seat, the comfort of her husband awaiting to soothe her.

"What do you mean?"

Tyler asked, turning the envelope in hand.

"We're moving to this town after all."

Kodi said, unexcitedly.

"Oh," Rebecca said, her voice between excitement and confusion.

"Thank you, Kodi. We've been busy securing a home in Olympus Cove near the north entrance." It was a newly developed neighborhood near the northern gates of the community. Tyler wasn't too familiar with it. Olympus Cove was utterly secluded, closed from the outside world, housing its schools, markets, and even a city council. But why would the Scotlers want to move here?

"We would love for you all to join us at our home, Becca," Diana added.

"Certainly," Rebecca replied. But it wasn't all music to Tyler's ears as he continued weighing upon whether to open the envelope, feeling a gnawing to know why now more than ever. What was everyone hiding from him? Each question unanswered felt like a piece of a jigsaw, elusive and challenging him to dig deeper.

"Well, we should be on our way," James said, standing from the couch again. Tyler, there is one more thing." James reached into his coat pocket. "Rebecca's told us of your need for a vehicle," he said, pulling out a single key. It's yours if you want it."

"That?" Tyler uttered, nodding toward the door as if the confines of walls didn't exist. "The car outside?" His voice teemed with confusion and an underline of excitement. He couldn't have been serious. "Aunt Rebecca?"

"James already asked. It's fine with us if you want it."

"I, I couldn't. I mean—we don't even know each other. Why give me a car?" Tyler answered back, his reply an attempt to gracefully refuse but feeling a combination of appreciation and confusion. Diana, Caleb, and Kodi finally joined James at the door, and just as abruptly as the strange family had arrived, they left the house. The air of the house changed with them gone. No one said anything; the silence of relief saturating the air.

Rebecca, composed during the visit from the Scotlers, seemed to have the jitters since their departure. Quick and abruptly, she cleaned up after everybody, setting the false bottle, and went to retrieve the half-emptied bottle Tyler picked up on the porch, the same bottle that triggered the weird and somewhat unsettling reaction in him for the first time. Tyler sat on the couch, watching her as she poured a glass and drank a few sips. He could observe her body visibly relaxing with each swallow. This simple thing, which was once so ordinary, now appeared strange.

The way she relished the drink, the immediate ease that washed over her—it raised a chilling suspicion. Could she be a creature of the night? The thought was outlandish, yet the past few weeks' events had stretched the boundaries of what

Tyler considered possible. Tyler's mind was wandering to new heights: the Scotler family, the twins, the glowing golden eyes, and their connection to his aunt and uncle. Could they, too, be more than they appeared? Were they part of a hidden world that Tyler was beginning to glimpse? And all the while, the puzzle pieces were slowly coming together—pieces that insinuated a far more complex and extraordinary reality than he had ever imagined.

As Tyler sat with the envelope in hand, remains of the visit from the Scotler family, so many questions unanswered, there seemed to grow an urge inside him: a necessity to discover the truth, no matter how unbelievable it might be.

CHAPTER SIX

THE BLIND SEARCH

That night, Tyler's dream unfolded in an image of a house: a villa perched on a cliff's edge, defyingly facing the extension of the landscape horizon. Windowless, it allowed the wind to dance through its halls with an unyielding freedom, carrying the scent of the distant sea. The dream was pulling him deeper into this new place, making him think about the surrounding elements. The wind grazed Tyler softly, like a caress against his skin; the structure and the infinite ethereal horizon it faced were surreal as Tyler walked towards an infinity pool of water that seemed to lead over the cliff's edge, meeting the horizon's embrace. He disturbed the pool's surface with his feet, feeling the cool liquid on his skin in sharp contrast to the warmth of the beating rays of the setting sun.

The clear liquid extended into nothingness below his feet and beckoned him to proceed. Very slowly, Tyler reached his fingertips to the surface of the liquid before plunging them into its depths, severing an ethereal tether to the dream world. Tyler woke with a start, and the feelings he had just experienced were carried with him as he wiped the moisture from his brow. It was something different from his usual terrors.

A distinct smell overwhelmed Tyler, pulling him out of his sheets and head. The scent of morning breakfast seduced him as he descended the stairs, but it strengthened in the dining room; spices and flavors danced at his nose—not the typical eggs and bacon. The night had been long, his mind restless, thoughts still tumbling with yesterday's events, the Scotler family, and the ethereal dream. The mystery of scents came undone as he sat at the table. A hearty breakfast of pancakes—but not just any pancakes, these were cooked with almonds and cinnamon and topped with fresh fruit—beside them lay well-spiced sausages, promising to taste as rich as they looked.

A meal Tyler hadn't seen Rebecca make in years. She came in from the kitchen carrying an array of condiments. Rion followed close behind her with glasses of OJ.

"What's the occasion?" Tyler asked.

"My apologies, of course," Rebecca replied, sincerely.

"I should have told you about the Scotlers and their reason for coming here sooner. It's time you knew."

As Tyler began to eat, savoring the flavors of his once-distant memory, he paused at Rebecca's words, his fork halfway to his mouth. Her face was serious, but a heavy knock on the front door rang out before she could continue. She startled and then put the bottles of flavored syrup and butter onto the table. "I've got it," Tyler pushed out his chair and moved towards the entrance, opening the door. Standing before him was a delivery man who professionally fought his expression of envious awe.

The sleek black car sat parked behind him on the street, where it had been the night before, only now it had been freshly polished, gleaming in the light of the dawning morning. "The keys, sir," the delivery man said, extending a small keyring towards him. "A gift from the Scotler family. They insisted it could not be refused."

Tyler's hand trembled as he took the keys, speechless. Before he could respond or thank the man, he nodded and walked away, leaving Tyler to his thoughts.

"Tyler, who's at the door?" Rebecca asked.

Tyler gazed at the delivery man and then the car: it was all an ostentatious display of wealth and a demonstration of how generous this family could be. He turned slowly with the key in his hand. "They had the car delivered." He ran his fingers around the cool metal of the key ring in disbelief. He looked up at his aunt and uncle, whose reactions were a mix of approval and amusement.

"James and Diana always had a flair for the extravagant," Rion remarked with a wide smile. Rebecca stood, meeting Tyler at the entrance and peering at the lavish car.

"It seems they have outdone themselves this time," she added, meeting Tyler's gaze again. She took his hands in hers, closing them around the key. "Accept this gift, or don't, but remember the gesture in which it is given. That should tell you all that you need. Make it a meaningful memory, not one focused on money." Tyler nodded, Rebecca's words hanging in the air. How could he ever repay such kindness? Should he accept the car? Maybe this was not just a gift; it was a challenge, a test of responsibility, and if it were, Tyler would rise to the occasion.

"I should go thank them in person," Tyler finally resolved, and the thought settled with a sense of purpose. As this determination took root, a second buzzing of Tyler's phone reminded him of his weekend commitments. A sudden realization that Kyle would be waiting for him after football practice. Tyler pulled the buzzing device out of his pocket, the rhythm accusingly indicating the time. Part of him wanted to stay and needed to hear what Rebecca would reveal, but there were other truths to be discovered. His gaze met Rebecca's once more. "Kyle's waiting for me," he said regretfully, "but can we talk about the Scotlers as soon as I get back?"

Rebecca nodded.

"Of course, do you want to drive your fancy new car?"

Hesitation flickered across Tyler's face like a shadow

moving over a sunlit path. The idea of being behind the wheel of such a luxury car was exhilarating yet scary. A tangle of nerves tightened in his stomach at the thought. "Should I?" he said. It wasn't so much a question as a statement, his voice blending awe and caution.

"Why not? It's yours to explore. What better way to start than a drive to school? A step towards new adventures to come." Rion answered from the dining table. With a deep breath, Tyler nodded, stepping into the world of responsibilities that awaited him.

"Alright."

*

Tyler was running late once again, keeping Kyle's waiting. He strolled across the school campus toward the stadium, still running high from his first drive in the car. The feel, every turn, and touch of the pedal—some strange tango with excitement and discovery. The sleek machine had moved like something alive, responding to Tyler's every command with intimidating precision.

By the time he parked his car, the nerves and excitement had left their marks, embedding it as a vivid memory of the freedom and responsibility he had been waiting for. The thoughts lingered in his mind as if it was all a dream as Tyler approached the stadium and spotted Kyle waiting. Brown hair askew from his football helmet lying at his feet, still in the scuffed shoulder gear and team jersey, engrossed in what he suspected to be a science textbook, consumed Kyle's full attention as he flipped its pages. "Hey, Ky!" Tyler called out, his voice breaking through the moment's tranquility. Kyle didn't look up from the book, a small smile on his face.

"No call, no texts, and you couldn't tell me you would be late again?" Kyle glanced up, meeting Tyler's gaze before returning to the open page. "Well, if you can be late, so can I. Wait while I finish this chapter," he added, waving Tyler off with a hand. Tyler smiled, shaking his head as he sat beside Kyle, confirming his suspicions—a science textbook.

"Don't you want to—"

"Almost done." Kyle urged.

Tyler kicked his feet up on the bench before them, patiently waiting. It wasn't long before Kyle flipped two or three more pages before closing the book and sighing as if the information he had just read had been confirmed in his brain. "So, what happened?"

Tyler hesitated, the words bubbling up in him like a pot of water on a hot stove, all too eager to come out. "For starters, remember that car we saw parked across the street from my house?" he began, putting one hand into his pocket and taking out the single key ring. Kyle's eyes widened, and he pushed the textbook away.

"No way. Seriously?" Tyler nodded as he continued retelling the story, coming undone from his lips like a banner in the wind. The story brought back waves of feelings: awe and disbelief, even a touch of fear and joy—all over again, each filling in the details of his still-reeling emotions. "What were they like?" Kyle asked, mouth still in awe.

"They're strange, more peculiar than I would have ever expected." Tyler's words trailed off, threading the key ring in his fingers. "I have to give the car back, right?"

Kyle shook his head, packing his textbook and removing his gear. "I mean, not necessarily. It was a gift. I'd keep it. But Tyler, what about your parents? Did they say anything about them?"

"Actually, yeah. Rebecca gave me this envelope. I took a photo of it." Tyler reached into his jacket pocket, pulled the device out, and showed Kyle the photo. "My parents told her to give it to me."

Kyle leaned closer, his eyes tracing the seal in the photo with the same mix of fascination and curiosity Tyler had when first seeing it. "What's inside of it?" he asked, his voice barely above a whisper, as if afraid to disturb the mysteries lingering in the photograph.

"I'm not sure," Tyler admitted, "I haven't opened it yet. The Scotlers suggested I wait until we meet at their new house." When Tyler said the words out loud to Kyle, it was evident that the Scotlers would be vital to uncovering his past. Kyle's eyes locked with Tyler's, and it was a silent pact between them, as though Tyler had thought of the idea, and Kyle was on board without words needing to be said. "We can look it up online and get some answers," Tyler proposed. It was their best idea to try to discover some of the truths within this garden of secrecy. "Think Ms. Frankel still opens the library for study hall on weekends?"

"Sure, she does, but wait a second, did you say new house?" Kyle replied.

*

Together, they were fast to the computer screens. Ms. Frankel did not mind the students having weekend studies. The students were always curious, though, why she spent her time working on an off day. The keyboard keys under Tyler's fingertips were an avenue to the realization of some clarity. It was more than a quest for answers; it was one to uncover deep connections tying Tyler to the past he was coming to know.

His fingers danced over the keys, calling up pages and pages of information. He skimmed results and articles until a headline in bold lettering caught his eye: *Rare Acquisition by Buyer Revitalizes Failing Auction House.*

It was dated just over six months ago.

Last Thursday, an extraordinary auction took place within the walls of A.A. Auction House. Centering around an item that has intrigued historians and collectors alike: a leather-bound book adorned with a peculiar symbol—a stylized "V" entangled with symbols. Latched from the outside, the book has never been opened by anyone…

His eyes were glued to the screen, taking in the article's points. The book was labeled a rare artifact of substantial historical importance and sold to a collector for an undisclosed amount. The purchaser, J.D.S., gave no other information. The sigil on the book was a royal lineage long thought dead, tied to myths and legends. Kyle came over to stand next to Tyler, peering over his shoulder with his eyes just as wide. "That's the same symbol on the envelope," he whispered.

"J.D.S.—James and Diana Scotler," Tyler added.

The sale not only revitalizes the struggling auction house but has also ignited a renewed interest in historical artifacts and their preservation. "It's a reminder," says Rachel Bedford, the current owner, "of the incredible stories that are hidden in plain sight, waiting to be rediscovered. This book is more than an artifact; it's a piece of history, a connection to a past that still holds many secrets."

"What if," Kyle ventured, a curious gleam in his eyes as Tyler turned to him, "we went to check out the Scotlers' house? Look for any weird clues?" The suggestion hung in the air as Tyler turned back to the screen, hesitant. His mind lacked the capacity to process any more information, let alone decipher the last couple of days. Yet, the pull of curiosity gnawed at him. The need to understand his history and ties was irresistible.

"Let's do it," Tyler decided, though his voice signaled otherwise, with a mixture of resolve and apprehension. "But we need to be careful. Our excuse will be me returning the car if we're caught. We don't know what we're walking into."

CHAPTER SEVEN

THE IMPARTIAL TRUTH

After the smooth ride, navigating the winding roads that led back to where he called home, Tyler pulled the new car into the familiar driveway, its engine purring softly into silence. The image of the book and its ancient symbol was still in his mind's eye, refusing to fade. He hesitated before leaving the car, torn between the yearning to sprint into the house and the dread of what he would hear—what Rebecca would have to say to him. With each step to the door, he wondered if she had known about the auction house sale or, in his mind, it seemed more like a reclaiming of a lost relic now. Maybe it truly was the Scotlers who bought the book? The thought sent shivers down his spine. Maybe his aunt was already solving the puzzle without him.

As he entered, the once familiar surroundings were teeming with a new weight of the unsaid and the unasked. A façade behind which lay answers to questions he had long waited to ask. And presently, the door of his room clicked softly behind him. He found everything normal in the embrace of these familiar walls.

Exhaling, he released a breath he hadn't even realized he was holding, and the tension unwound as he dropped to the floor, leaning his back against the bed frame. An open notebook lay beside his bed from when he had been catching up with overdue English homework. But here he was, at last, sitting under the glow of a screen as his phone cast light on his face, in thought. Composing his text message to Kyle, he thought about his previous offer to visit the construction site of the Scotler house. *"When should we go?"* His sent message returned with a buzz seconds later.

"We can just drive by. No hardcore snooping. No one will see us." Kyle replied.

Tyler sighed and replied carefully, "*All right. I'll pick you up on the way.*"

He sighed again and tossed the phone beside himself before picking it and the notebook and heading downstairs. His determination was cut short as he ran into his aunt and uncle entering from the kitchen. "Where are you running off to, Tyler? Dinner is almost ready," asked Rebecca, with a towel over her shoulder.

Rion stood beside her.

"Going out for a drive with Ky. I'll be back before dinner," Tyler replied.

"At least before curfew. Drive safe in that fancy car of yours," Rion reminded him, Rebecca nodding in agreeance as Tyler reached the entrance.

"I will!" He replied, the door shutting behind him. He looked out into the cool evening sky, the brushstrokes of twilight tones painted in streaks of vibrant oranges and purples as the sun fell on the night. Another exhale, and he was ready.

It was another quiet drive with Kyle into the new neighborhood. Tyler caught glimpses of the new neighborhood as he drove. Anything but the usual scenes flashed by: a place of possibility, of construction—underlined by the secrets that lay in the shadows around their town. The air filled with anticipation. The scattered, big, empty houses made the neighborhood a ghost town in the making: a place of dreams and wealth frozen in the middle of becoming a reality.

Several structures stood half-complete, with their skeletal frames standing in testimony to the aspirations of those who dreamed them up. Some streets held no life and were full of potential, resembling the cyclone of questions and possibilities that swirled around in Tyler's mind. "These houses are crazy. Which one is theirs?" Kyle asked as they rounded a winding corner.

Before them, a house unlike any other they had seen in the neighborhood came into view. It was an actual mansion with a big garden lining the corner, embraced by wilderness and surrounding forestry. Its landscaping was meticulous and deliberate, blending untamed beauty with structured design elegance. Large windows punctuated its façade, offering glimpses of the interior, while the well-lit entryway beckoned them closer, a beacon in the twilight. Tyler parked the car on the other side of the dimly lit street, the engine's purr dying to silence as they both looked out; he and Kyle marveling at the magnificence. "Well, looks like they've moved in already," Kyle said.

Tyler said nothing and looked outside the house. The inside was all dark and quiet; the house itself seemed hollow. However, something seemed to move out of the corner of his eye at the forest's edge. The dense undergrowth along the line of the property throbbed with the chatter of the invisible. At that moment, Tyler squinted and tried to make out what he was moving in the shadows. Abruptly breaking the stillness of the night, a sharp knock at Tyler's window resounded, and his heart pounded, and he and Kyle sprang to attention. As he turned, they confronted the figure of a man by the window, wrapped in a long black coat, yet it appeared to drink the last rays of daylight.

"Good evening, Tyler," he said, the sound of his deep baritone reaching through the glass. It was James Scotler. Tyler opened the window, merging the space between them.

"Mr. Scotler, hello," he stuttered with heavy breath.

"Good to see you, and—" he trailed off, his piercing gaze drifting to Kyle.

"Kyle Huntington, sir," Kyle said quickly.

"Of course, pleasure to make your acquaintance, Kyle." The tension in the air was palpable, rolling in like a heavy bowling ball. It gave Tyler goosebumps, thinking about getting caught trespassing, crossing that invisible line, his palms so sweaty that he could barely stay gripping the steering wheel. At the same time, Tyler and Kyle sent nervous glances back and forth across the hood at one another, wordlessly communicating a shared apprehension, a tangible force holding them together in the moment.

They had been the trespassers, the intruders on the brink of the unknown, dangling right at the edge of discovery. But they had been caught in the act; their intentions laid bare to James, the unexpected observer. His nerves were twisted tight in the moment, stretched thin by the suspense; he couldn't help but feel that he and Kyle were all too aware of the consequences of their actions at the mercy of the city council—or worse, under the watch of their guardians. "Is there something I could—" James started, his voice steady, a needle to the aired balloon of tension between them.

"I came to return the car. It was a nice gesture, but I can't accept it." Tyler said in a panic. The words tumbled out of his mouth faster than they formed in his mind. Kyle glanced over, suspected, a look of surprise on his face at Tyler's quick thinking, sticking to the plan. Tyler turned slowly to James, their gaze meeting. James smiled, letting out a soft chuckle in steam as his warm breath met the cooled evening air.

"I see. Then how were you two planning to get home?" He replied. Tyler was dumbfounded. A clear hole in his plan he hadn't thought of an excuse for. He opened his mouth for a moment, hopeful the words would once again pour out, but nothing did. Instead, he smiled, a guilty smile of defeat. "Keep the car, at least for a while longer. Return here in a month with your guardians and join us for dinner. We should be moved in fully by then." In a kneejerk reaction, Tyler nodded with a hard swallow.

"Whoa, did you see that?" Kyle said, snatching Tyler's

attention away with something in the forest's depths. Tyler turned to catch the tall trees in the distance, swaying in the light breeze, their leaves rustling, and then, for a mere heartbeat, a pair of golden-glowing eyes piercing the darkness. Tyler leaned forward at the edge of his seat but was restrained by his seatbelt, which was still buckled in. James said nothing at first, seemingly unfazed by the sudden interruption.

"Something in the forest? A wild animal, perhaps." He said, his voice calm as the night. Given the untamed wilderness surrounding the newly erected structure, it was a plausible explanation. "The area has been untouched by humans for quite some time," he added with a dismissive wave of his hand.

"Sure," Tyler replied, his gaze locked on the forestry.

"You both should get home. It's getting late." James said, his calm voice laced with stern instruction. Tyler stared at the forest for a few minutes longer before heading the words and igniting the car's engine. Kyle was also locked onto the sight, awaiting movement in the trees. James backed from the car as Tyler pulled away slowly, a glance in the rearview mirror offering a final glimpse of the mysterious James Scotler. Hands in his coat pockets, his figure an imposing silhouette against the luminous moonlit night. Another glance, in the span of a breath, and he was gone. Leaving only the empty space where he stood.

"There's something weird about that guy, right?" Kyle asked. Tyler nodded slowly as the car glided down the quiet road. The evening had sown more seeds of suspicion in his mind: the house, its nature, and James Scotler's presence.

"Did you see the eyes in the woods too?" Tyler asked.

"I'm not sure what I saw. There was a figure, sort of like before, but not." Kyle replied, "You aren't going to join them for dinner, are you?"

Tyler shrugged. "You don't think I should?"

"I don't know, Ty. James seemed—his energy was intense, is all." As the car hummed through the darkened streets, the atmosphere inside was thick with the residual adrenaline of the encounter. From the moment of the knock at the window, Tyler's mind was a frantic panic of curiosity and caution. The idea of attending dinner with his Aunt Rebecca seemed it could dilute any truths spoken. Would she try protecting him from the truth? "James is intense," Tyler at last said, "the whole family is, but I think I should go alone." The car's idled engine now purred in the driveway of Kyle's home.

"Just let me know if you do decide to tell them." Kyle said, exiting the car, "Oh, and this car is sick. You should definitely keep it." Kyle added, dragging a hand along the door panel. When Tyler arrived home and entered, the comforting aroma of a hot meal greeted him at the door. "Just in time," Rebecca said, placing plates on the table. The normalcy of the scene was a grounding reminder of Tyler's growing double life—one foot in the mundane, the other stepping into the unknown. Smiling, he flung himself into a chair at the dinner table. "Your uncle should be down shortly." She added, placing another plate down.

"Ky and I saw James Scotler tonight." The words tumbled out of his mouth again in a way that shocked Tyler himself; he hadn't meant for it to sound quite so blunt, even forceful.

"Oh?" Rebecca froze in surprise and contemplation, her face momentarily registering the shock of the news before composing itself into an unreadable mask.

"Yes. Kyle and I drove by the new development, saw their house, and he was there." Tyler added, studying his aunt's face. Her lips tightened as if weighing words behind them. As the silence stretched, a creak from the staircase announced Rion's arrival. He entered casually, greeting them with a nod before noticing the stale atmosphere.

"What's all the serious faces for?" he asked, seamlessly integrating himself into the conversation as he sat at the table.

"Earlier, Rebecca mentioned wanting to tell me something about the Scotlers. Why they were in town? And the envelope you both kept a secret?" Tyler probed. Rebecca exchanged a quick glance with Rion, a muted conversation passing between them before she answered.

"The Scotlers are here because I asked them to come," she began, her voice steady but laced with something unspoken, regret perhaps, or something else. "I didn't expect them to move here so quickly, though. As for the envelope," she paused, her gaze drifting as if the mention of it held a weight beyond its physical existence. "It contains a family heirloom."

Tyler's brow furrowed as his interest deepened with questions about the envelope's significance, which led his aunt to ask the Scotlers to come to Olympus Cove. "Wait, what kind of heirloom? And why did you ask them to come?" he asked, confusion and interest lacing his tone. Rion cleared his throat before speaking.

"We thought it was time you knew them. It's what Aiden and Alina would have wanted," he said, his voice carrying solemn notes. "They were very close to your family."

The vague answers only fueled Tyler's frustration. "Why now, though?" he pressed, desperate for clarity in the maze of half-answers and secrets. Neither Rebecca nor Rion answered right away, their evasiveness wrapped in the guise of doing what's best for him without revealing the true depth of their intentions.

"This will all make sense soon, we promise." Rebecca finally answered. Left with more questions than answers yet again, Tyler made a silent vow to himself: if the truth was not going to be given freely, he'd get it even if it meant he had to take it. The envelope, sitting on the top of his dresser in his bedroom now, was the key to unlocking all the secrets lurking around him. Regardless of the envelope's contents, he would open it and find the truth his way.

CHAPTER EIGHT
THE HONEST SEEKER

It was almost three weeks since Tyler attempted to open what once belonged to his late parents. He stood in his bedroom that night after dinner, alone with the weight of the sealed envelope in hand—a piece of the past, a mystery, a secret handed down to him by Rebecca. It made him feel like it was almost sacred, the wax seal a gateway to truths about his family. Yet, as his fingers toyed with the edges of the seal, the sharp edges of the aged paper, hovering on the threshold of breaching such secrets, an eerie hush fell over the room. Out of the silence came faint, ghostly whispers, male and female voices intertwining, threading through the air.

Swirling about him, their murmurs approached…*the key to close. The key to waking…*the voices stilled his hands…*the one who is royal, the one who should wait…*the voices were otherworldly, fraught with some kind of emotion Tyler couldn't quite put his finger on. They felt as if they came from the very walls that once echoed in happiness and joy of the life he knew before the Scotler family arrived. The decision not to open the envelope his parents left behind lay heavy on his heart. Abandoning the choice to open the envelope meant leaving its contents veiled until it was time.

***

As the last bell of the school week rang, a palpable sense of relief reverberated through the hallways, meaning another weekend had begun. Yet for Tyler, when classes let out this particular Friday, it was more than a release from academics but an entrance into an evening of expectation. The upcoming dinner with the Scotler family is at the top of his mind. Tyler made his way through the halls with the eager hustle of students, ready to evade the grasp of the school. Seeing one of his peers leaving the same history classroom that provoked the outlandish theories from the class brought back that faithful question he could not shake—*creatures of the night*, or possibly more appropriately, the creatures Phoenix wrote about in the articles. Tyler's steps led him to the classroom. Inside stood Mr. Witwer amidst the lingering aura of lessons given.

Tyler paused for a second before asking the question aloud that had been lipping inside him, "Mr. Witwer, I have a question for you concerning the creatures of the night," Tyler took another step forward as Mr. Witwer glanced up from an open notebook at his desk, "have you ever seen the online writings of Phoenix concerning various creatures?"

The question hung in the air for a moment.

Mr. Witwer's expression was thoughtful before resting on realization. "Yes, I've heard of the articles," he replied. "But take the articles with a grain of salt. The author, Phoenix, was known to stir trouble with their theories." He added. Tyler ignored the warning, pushing on, too driven by his quest to find answers.

"Do you think there is any truth to the claims? What about creatures with glowing golden eyes?" His questions had risen above academia, a clear quest for understanding, a necessity to know if the shadows dancing at the fringes of his reality were imbued with fact or fantasy spun by Phoenix. Tyler's teacher met his gaze with further intrigue, removing his glasses.

"It's possible, but Tyler, I don't understand. Have you seen something?" he inquired. Tyler shifted uncomfortably, clinging to his backpack straps as he suddenly realized he may have spoken too much. The room felt like it shrank five sizes, the air charged with caution. Admitting to the truth, confessing his own suspicions and sightings—the impossible—felt like stepping into a chasm from which there was no return.

However, to deny it meant becoming someone he was not. "Just curiosity," Tyler finally managed, his voice a soft whisper, "I've always found the ideas…fascinating." Mr. Witwer studied him for a moment longer, his eyes softening as if he recognized the delicate dance of truth and secrecy.

"Curiosity," he started, "…is the lantern by which we

navigate the unknown. But know that not all that is hidden seeks to be found." Tyler nodded and started out of the room, thinking of what his teacher said. A reminder that some truths, once revealed, can never be buried again. It wasn't long before Tyler found himself standing before the grand estate, more elaborate than when he and Kyle first saw it, which Tyler had taken to calling Scotler Manor.

With each heartbeat and step down the stone path toward the enormous double doors, Tyler felt the air thrum with anticipation. More than anticipation, an ancient force older than the stars themselves, the envelope in his backpack an anchor of focus. When he reached for the doors, it was as though the structure recognized its visitor, an unseen force opening the doors to welcome Tyler. He felt a breathless excitement as he stood at the threshold, at the edge of that thinning boundary that drew a line of division between truth and secrets.

"Good evening, Tyler," Diana's silky tone instantly soothed him as she emerged from behind the large door with a welcoming smile.

"Good evening, Mrs. Scotler," he said, stepping over the threshold onto the shiny marble floors of the foyer. The house opened through the doorway into soaring ceilings that felt like they touched the sky. It was even larger inside than Tyler had ever imagined. Arches surrounded the entry in all directions, making it hard for Tyler to know where to look first. Dangling from the high ceilings were stunning crystal chandeliers shimmering in natural and man-made light.

Below the dazzle of the chandeliers was a vast array of exquisite furniture scattered about the space. In the middle of that sprawl was a grand staircase, a marvel of design that spiraled ever onward as though it had been sculpted by some force to reach another plane and buffed to a sheen surpassing even that of the sun itself. The most spectacular sight Tyler had ever beheld.

"Dinner will be ready shortly. Please, join us."

Swallowed by the magnificence around him, Tyler followed his usherer, Diana. The next room was even more awe-gazing than the first. His shock melted into a sinking despair. In the flicker of another even more enormous chandelier were Rebecca and Rion conversing casually with James. "Hello, Tyler," James called out upon entering. Tyler's eyes darted around the room as though homing in on eyes fixated on him. Rebecca and Rion stood by the white marble mantle, James next to them, and one of the twins, Tyler wasn't sure which, was seated on a vast white couch.

Finally, Tyler's eyes landed on his guardians, their expressions unwavering and, to his surprise, not scolding. Tyler would have even gone so far as to say that he saw a slight smile beginning to edge in at the corner of Rebecca's mouth. "Join us," Rebecca said, gesturing Tyler to a nearby armchair.

As Tyler crossed the room, Diana stood at the archway to another room. "Caleb is helping me in the kitchen. Kodi, will you join us? Dinner will be served shortly." She said, leaving the room with Kodi following closely behind her. The room fell silent upon their departure, aside from the distant echoes of clinking dishes through the archway. Instead, the silence was filled with awkwardness. Tyler felt awkward enough sitting in the expensive and extremely comfortable white armchair.

A common theme of Scotler Manor, even the walls were pure, untouched, and sterile looking. His instincts screamed that he should not have been sitting in the chair. He sat with his head low for a moment as if waiting for his punishment.

"We aren't upset with you, Tyler," Rion said, his voice gentle. Tyler looked up to meet his gaze. He crossed the room, kneeling beside the armchair, Rebecca behind her husband with a comforting hand on his uncle's shoulder.

"James called us. We don't understand why you wouldn't have told us." Rebecca started, "We've always encouraged honesty in this family," her voice warm but resting on the seriousness of her words. "Though I suppose we haven't been entirely truthful with you ourselves. We understand you wanting the truth, but isolating yourself from those who care about you could put you in unnecessary danger, Tyler."

Tyler shifted in his chair; then his gaze fell to his hands before he spoke. "I just thought this was something I had to do alone. To prove I could handle the truth, whatever it may be—what kind of danger?" Tyler looked up. As he met Rebecca's gaze again, her mouth open to speak, Diana appeared through the archway.

"Dinner is served," she announced. They stood up, Rion's reassuring hand at Tyler's back as they went. The air grew slightly more relaxed as they moved toward the dining room. The magnificence continued to the dinner table as Tyler entered.

A man stood behind a long stone island slab. His fingers laced together before him. Dressed in a long, black chef's hat and apron, he nodded at Tyler as Diana ushered the group. The table was another giant slab of grey stone. Set with various dishes nestled within various plants and fruits, plates perfectly positioned, and delicate-looking glasses placed at each.

Diana led Tyler to an empty seat.

He didn't dare put his hands on the spread, interlacing them in his lap as he sat. "Tonight, we've prepared for you braised wagyu steak with a special sauce of Chef Hans' for our guests of honor," Diana announced before taking her seat beside James. Tyler felt himself turn red. It was all too much. Though the room's atmosphere was lighter, the underlying current of their earlier conversation remained. A sign that the conversation was far from over.

Tyler nodded and smiled, thanking the chef before turning to Caleb, who sat opposite him.

"Do you always eat like this?"

Caleb chuckled. "Yeah, kind of," he replied.

Tyler glanced at his aunt and uncle, who seemed unaffected by the sight before them as they chatted casually. Tyler looked at the spread again, his hand slowly pulling out from under the table, finger gently tracing the high-end silverware at his place. He looked around the room to see the Scotler family cutting into their steaks, though they were much rarer than Tyler was used to. Tyler was surprised that even his aunt and uncle were sharing the meal.

Tyler cut into his own anyway, taking a small bite. The flavors of the meat he tasted were foreign, like nothing he had ever tasted; savory and tender, they danced on his tongue and sang songs to his taste buds. The only note he could not ignore was its raw metallic iron essence. His instinctual reaction was to chase the bite with a forkful of vegetables and sides, hoping to overpower it.

"Thank you for joining us tonight," James said.

"I've been looking forward to it," said Tyler, around a mouthful of more vegetables. Even as he was saying the words, he could feel the knot forming in his throat with the next swallow, trying to get through another bite and wanting to skip the pleasantries. "James," he started, patting at the corners of his mouth with the angel cloud of a napkin beside his plate, "what can you tell me about my parents?" Asking had been easier than he thought, even though the question hung like iron-clad armor.

"Tyler," Rebecca warned sternly.

The air thickened within the dining room at the sound of it. Sensing the shift, the chef moved swiftly, whisking away plates while tension gripped the room. "Tyler, Rebecca, would you join me in the study?" James's voice cut through the silence. Tyler lifted his gaze from the remains on his plate, his steak still intact. The lighthearted expression Rebecca wore melted away, revealing a face of anticipation as she rose.

"Dinner was a delight, Diana. Thank you," Rebecca said in that way she had of adding weight to her voice, which made clear the seriousness of the night ahead. Diana gave an enclosed smile, but her eyes thanked her. Tyler swallowed the last of his drink and got up, following James and Rebecca as they left. He walked out with a last, long look back over his shoulder at Caleb, Kodi, Diana, and Rion. Steady eyes as he watched the silent exchanges and the undercurrent of unease that now filled the room.

Walking into the room he had been in earlier, Tyler picked up his backpack from beside the chair. As he ascended the grand staircase, Tyler felt his heart thumping with exhilaration. Was it finally happening? Would he finally get the answers he sought? Each step down the corridor felt like a step into a new life, leaving behind what was. Elegant pendants lighted the corridor, their reflective glow dancing on the floors below them.

Reaching the study's door revealed an office where knowledge hung heavy, almost a palpable presence. Books of all sizes and ages climbed the walls, with wooden ladders on metal tracks against them, hinting at worlds beyond his own. The room was bathed in the soft glow of another chandelier. The bookshelves framed the room, leading to a large glass window that offered a view of the manor's sprawling backyard and the courtyard below. The moonlight streamed through the glass, casting a silver glow that danced on the top of a desk placed before it.

Rebecca sat in an armchair in the center of the room. James leaned against the wooden desk. It was a modern take on something fit for the Oval Office. Tyler practically bounded onto the compact couch opposite the armchair in the room, tossing his backpack onto the floor beside him with a thud. Across from him, Rebecca and James exchanged a glance before Rebecca's voice broke the heavy silence.

"Almost everyone loved our family," she started, her voice a soft, earnest murmur, "Your parents, they loved you more than the stars love the night sky." Feeling a sudden tightness in his chest, Tyler turned over his shoulder to James, seeking some sort of anchor as Rebecca's words trailed into the shadows. James went to the large window, staring out into the distance.

"But not all eyes that watched your family did so with

kindness. Some…some wished to see the light of your family extinguished." James said solemnly. Tyler's heart raced as he pivoted back to Rebecca, noticing her head dip as if the burden of her next words would be too heavy.

"Extinguished? What do you mean? What happened to them?" Tyler pressed desperately.

"There are things you won't fully understand right now—but know that this family has an extraordinary legacy," Rebecca replied softly as if whispers of secrets were in the air.

James came back to the wooden desk. He opened a drawer, revealing an object that caught Tyler's eye—there it was, the book, the one he had seen in the online article from the auction house. Its allure magnified here in the flesh, the symbol on its cover glowing under the moonlight that flowed through the window. "This journal," James proclaimed, "was also saved for you, intended for the day you were ready to bear its truths." Tyler moved closer, some force, not his own, compelling him, and his fingers moved over the embossed symbol, the strap, and the lock that kept the secrets of the past.

Tyler sat at the desk, book before him, when Rebecca

joined him with the comforting warmth of her presence. "Tyler, what I wanted to tell you before was that your family history is woven of light and shadow. I asked James to bring this book because you're old enough now that things will start to make more sense," she said, meeting Tyler's gaze, a hand on his arm. Did you bring the envelope?" Tyler nodded, craning his head over his shoulder to the couch. He stood, retrieving the envelope from his backpack, and returned to the desk with it, holding it for a moment before breaking the wax seal. The latch on the book opened the moment Tyler broke the seal. He could see a silver ring inside the envelope etched with symbols on its surface.

"This ring has been passed down for years."

Rebecca said.

Handling the ring with care, the cover of the book suddenly flew open, and Tyler began to read its text...*the royal family has kept its secrets for far too long*...the book's entries didn't make sense...*it is the eve of battle, the kingdom fears this will be our last night. The Cerif are coming...where are our Shafeir guardians when we need them most?* The words on the page bled like ink smeared off the edges of the book. Tyler flipped past a few blank pages to another entry, names of people he had never heard of, and then names he did recognize…*Aiden and Alina have escaped. The Vasilikós bloodline shall live on… be forever grateful…*

"What—is this? Am I supposed to believe this?" Tyler asked, looking up from the pages, his voice full of skepticism. James and Rebecca exchanged another glance, nodding, "Cerif, Shafeir, and Vasi—"

"Vasilikós," Rebecca answered, completing the sentence.

"The royal family, the most powerful of us," James added, sinking back into the chair.

"Us?" Tyler asked, his voice still stained with disbelief.

"The Vasili are a royal bloodline, born with gifts in their veins. You are a direct descendant of that bloodline, Tyler." James added. Tyler struggled to wrap his head around the revelation—it was a mistake. Royal? But before he could manage to get his words out, Rebecca continued, "The Scotlers are Shafeir, guards of the royal Vasilikós created by the ancient Vasili blood and—" A moment of opportunity arose as she trailed off.

Tyler shook his head.

The concept felt alien, a stark contrast to the life he's known. "We aren't royal. I'm not royalty. Look at our lives compared to theirs," he gestured to James and the extravagant room they sat in, "if anything, they're royalty." Tyler said, his voice firm.

"The royal family created us many centuries ago to serve as guardians. As for our fortune, trust that you share in it. It was decided that keeping you hidden would mean leaving anything of suspicion behind." James replied. Tyler sank into his chair, his thoughts consuming him. Rebecca was quiet for a moment, confronting her own thoughts.

"So much has been hidden from you for your protection. But the royal blood flows through you, Tyler. The legacy of the Vasili, it's your birthright." She whispered.

"If we're royal, then where is our kingdom?" Tyler asked, still wrestling with disbelief and a growing sense of destiny. Questions of kingdoms lost, and foes lurking were dizzying.

"Far from this place," James replied, "the Cerif, however,

have taken it."

"Right, right, and what are the Cerif exactly?"

Tyler probed.

The room was silent as each word stitched Tyler more and more into the tapestry of a world he'd only just begun to become aware of. When James spoke next, his voice had changed, the words barbed in venom and sorrow. "Cerif are beings who crave power. They seek out those who would oppose them and go to any length possible to sway those they deem worthy of their cause. That's why we've come for you, Tyler. We suspect they will come for you next, now that you are of ruling age." The whirling in Tyler's mind turned dizzying as the final words of revelation James spoke hung in the air like a spell, a pang in his stomach settling in with nausea. Tyler felt the room tilt like the ground beneath his feet was warping.

"I think I'm going to be sick," Tyler said, pulling back from the desk, book, and ring. A surge of dizziness washed over him. Rebecca was quickly by his side as Tyler stood, placing a trembling hand on his head. He struggled to anchor himself amidst the storm brewing inside. Seconds later, Diana and the twins entered the study.

"What happened? Are you alright, Tyler?"

Diana asked.

Concern was sewn within Rebecca's voice as it cut through the fog of disbelief Tyler felt. "He's not feeling well," she told everybody, but her words barely penetrated the hurricane that raged inside Tyler. It was a far-off fairy tale, too fantastic to be part of his world. But it was no simple tale of knights and dragons. All this weight of lineage and power claimed to run through his veins, the hidden truths of his family—all crashing into him like a tidal wave, leaving him gasping for breath in its wake.

"I must be dreaming," he whispered, trying desperately to make sense of the impossible. But the room was still spinning, the ground beneath his feet moving in and out of reality as quickly as myth. And then the world around him grew dim, the figures of his aunt, the wooden desk, and the Scotlers before him fading into lost shadows. Tyler felt his strength drain from his body like a vessel emptied of its essence. In response, he gave in to the darkness, and his consciousness slid into nothing.

The last image he saw was Diana, with piercing golden glowing eyes, coming toward him and the sound of James's voice, his words echoing in his ears. "We must be careful now."

CHAPTER NINE

THE TRUTH TELLER

Man 1: When darkness fades, it leaves behind a residue of the past. Before the breaking of dawn, we must fight the long night on.

"What?" Tyler mumbled as his consciousness drifted back; somewhere in the back of his head, there seemed to echo a very slight, faint voice, a whisper from the void that claimed him. The gentle heat of the sun enveloped him, an embrace draped over his skin, cradling him within the tender sanctity of a bed not his own, then remembering in the haze what came before falling to blackness. Memories flitted back in disjointed flashes: the rush in his head, the book and the ring, and the haunting image that lingered at the edge of his consciousness—golden glowing eyes of Diana Scotler, piercing and enigmatic.

"What was that, Tyler? I'm here." When Tyler finally opened his eyes, he saw Rebecca at his bedside; her voice was gentle, and her face was drenched in concern. In the aftermath of revelations that felt more like riddles, Tyler awoke to a world that seemed intimately familiar and unsettlingly foreign. His eyes wandered wildly. Judging from the surroundings, he was still at Scotler Manor. Much like the rest of the home, this room was exquisitely furnished, full of abstract paintings that decorated the walls and big windows to accept the flooding sunlight. Soft murmurs from the silhouettes in the distance caught Tyler's eye in the doorway; James, Diana, Rion, and the twins were all there. Their conversation ceased as Tyler sat up in the cushioned bed, his head still spinning.

"How are you feeling, Tyler?" Diana asked, crossing the room. The others followed.

"I'm not sure," answered Tyler, flipping through his senses. Looking down, he could see the ring around his index finger—a piece of the past—shining, reflecting the sunlight on its surface.

"I thought you might want to wear it," Rebecca said softly. Uncertainty knotted in Tyler's chest as he eyed the ring. He wasn't sure what he wanted anymore. He thought he wanted the truth. Part of him still did, but he needed time to process it all. Diana's voice cut through his contemplations as she sat opposite Rebecca on the edge of the bed.

"Your eyes," Tyler started, meeting Diana's gaze.

"Yes. What you saw was real. James tells me you are finding this all difficult to believe. Know this: what you have been told is the truth; what you read in that journal is real. James and Rebecca could have been gentler in their approach, but unfortunately, time is not on our side." Diana's voice was stringent, but her accent softened the words into a gentle blow. "My eyes are those of a Shafeir; when we turn to our vampiric gifts, they often change hue."

"Vampiric gifts?" Tyler repeated in a whisper.

"Don't worry about that right now," Rebecca interjected.

There was no way Tyler was about to argue. He couldn't

process anything else at the moment. He wiped a hand over his face as though he were trying to wipe away the questions that kept climbing into his brain. "All right, we'll leave you alone to rest," Diana surrendered as the room started emptying again, leaving Tyler with his thoughts and the ring that now felt like a question mark on his finger. He stared at the ring, thumbing it between his fingers.

The room offered nothing in terms of answers, the silence becoming a contemplative space. Tyler felt drawn to the ring; with all the carvings, it was smoother than he expected, as if thumbing it might reveal secrets on its own. The world he knew was coming apart at the seams, and in its place, a new reality whispered, fraught with magic and mysteries he was only beginning to glimpse. He thought of his disbelief in the wake of the revealed truth: he needed something or someone familiar to him with so much unfamiliarity.

He needed to talk to Kyle.

*

Kyle was the one person who always anchored Tyler in reality. Their text message exchange was a lifeline, though Tyler withheld the whole truth for fear of tampering with their relationship, the one ordinary connection he desperately needed. Besides, admitting to his new reality felt like an acceptance he wasn't ready to give, a surrender to a world that felt too fantastical to embrace. When Kyle offered his help, Tyler was lost in a paradox of his desires. Wanting to be pulled from the abyss of discovery that was claiming him. The truth was a double-edged sword, and Tyler stood pressed against its end, wondering if he was ready. Tyler reflected on what lay ahead in the room's silence with the moon as his witness.

The truth, once sought, now weighed heavy in his hands. Was he ready to accept it—to step into the legacy that called to him from the shadows? Only time would tell, but for now, he knew he must at least try to understand the world that opened before him. He was in a world where the past and the present were becoming interlaced and a house where secrets whispered in the dark promised to reshape everything he thought he knew. He began responding to Kyle: *I need to know more about this ring. Can you do some research?*

Tyler slid the ring from his finger with a sense of urgency, capturing its intricate details in a photo nestled in his palm. He sent it off into the digital ether, and his message was quickly acknowledged with a read receipt. Tyler's gaze remained fixed on his phone, anticipation and anxiety in his throat as he awaited a response that, for agonizing moments, didn't come. Just as the pulsing typing indicators sparked a glimmer of hope, a voice sliced through, derailing Tyler's focus.

"Tyler, are you all right?"

It was Rebecca entering the room. As she sat down next to him, the remaining traces of her grief were present—the crushed tissue in her hand evidence she was upset.

"What's wrong?" Tyler asked, putting down his digital lifeline. The way Rebecca hesitated, her following words sounded heavy.

"I didn't want you to find out like this." After all the years spent with Rebecca and the evasion of his questioning, Tyler knew now that he would finally hear the truth. He was preparing himself for what she would say.

"I don't even know how many years it's been…" She tugged down the collar of her sweater to reveal the bulging of veins and the wrinkling of her skin—the wear of years had begun descending her arm. "The accelerated aging began just after you entered high school. The bottles coming to the house were all from James, a special blend of—blood."

Tyler's heart sank. His mind raced as he pieced together her words and the fragments of the words he read by writer *Phoenix, the creatures of the night* all rushing to the forefront of his mind. It was true—the fabric of the ordinary ripped away, the threads of the supernatural exposed. He found himself recoiling away from her touch. That nauseous feeling returned to his gut. "The animals in the woods, the creatures of the night," he said in a mumble of panic. "What are you, Rebecca? I don't understand." The alarm in his voice getting louder.

"No, Tyler. It's not what you think. James' blood, the blood of a Shafeir, sustains me."

"Like a vampire? What are all of you?" Tyler urged again.

Rebecca steadied her voice before answering, "The Shafeir are hybrids created from Vasili and True Vampire blood.

They do not harm—I do not harm innocents. The Shafeir are protectors."

"That doesn't answer my question, what are you? Were my parents True—"

"No," Rebecca snapped, "the Vasili are no vampires of any kind. Though they are powerful beings. I am stuck somewhere between human and something more. The Shafeir are afforded the option of consuming blood or sustaining on food and, of course, walking in daylight. True Vampires must feed on the living essence and live in the shadows. I have lived quite a long life because of what is known as Gifted Blood— the blood of a gifted being, be it Vasili or Shafeir. Shafeir blood sustains me mostly now, but it isn't as pure—not as pure as the royal Vasili blood your mother and father used to provide me."

"And if you required their blood, and now James', that would mean you aren't—" Tyler's chest tightened again, his heart pounding in his ears as he trailed off, the thought becoming crystal clear. Rebecca wiped her tearful eyes and cleared her throat.

"Yes, I was adopted into the family many years ago." Tyler's world shifted on its axis, and the puzzle pieces clicked with chilling clarity. A bond born not by blood but by necessity—leaving Tyler to wrestle with the weighty legacy of secrecy and sacrifice. In this realization, his feeling of things came upon him with the closing shadows of night pressing through the room's walls, sandwiching him between disbelief and destiny. The ring on his finger, a heritage calling him, and his aunt's honesty sat before him, guiding him toward truths that promised to rearrange his existence—questioning who he could trust and what he was supposed to do now.

CHAPTER TEN

THE PROTECTOR

It seemed time had slipped through Tyler's fingers like grains of sand; the middle of the week arrived with the abruptness of a thunderclap. Back in his familiar surroundings of the place he called home and the comfort of his bed. He missed two days of school, a minor concern, but it still bothered him. And there was no sign of Kyle, who appeared to be the last unchanging thing in his life, the one certainty he could count on, and he was missing. No messages, no calls, nothing. It was unlike him. Where was he?

Tyler lay motionless in bed as the light of dawn crept through the curtains. It had only been days since the revelation that his aunt, who had raised him all his life, was bound to him and his family not by blood but by choices—and her life sustained by theirs. That alone rocked the foundation of his world. Still, the revelations continued tumbling down like an avalanche—his claim to royalty, which was still too incredible and sounded like it was pulled out from the books he read as a boy, vampires, creatures of the night, and nightmares, fiction realized, his connection to a world where such beings existed. Even worse, the Scotler family, their enigmatic smiles, lavish gifts, and eyes that seemed to know too much, were all Shafeir hybrids.

Amidst his inner turmoil, getting ready for school today felt alien. Alien as it was, Tyler found a semblance of normalcy in this routine, if only for a moment, a tether to the world he once knew. He was soon nearing the too-out-of-place car gift from the Scotler family. The cool morning air brushed at his skin from the window while sitting in the car. As he drove to school, Tyler felt the total weight of his new reality. How would he go out into the daylight, into the ordinary world, with such extraordinary secrets shadowing his every step?

Pulling into the parking lot, the car's engine a low purr before settling in silence. Tyler sat for a moment, his phone in hand, hopeful to see a response from Kyle, but he hadn't. Drifting in thought, his gaze fell to his hand, the lustrous ring still coiling his finger, reflecting streams of sunlight in a pattern that danced back in his eyesight. Its markings were so distinct, with twelve symbols around the band. His curiosity led him back to Kyle and the lingering message. Where was he? It would be him if anyone could find information on something so ancient. Tyler needed to find Kyle today. He needed the help of his friend.

His footsteps echoed as Tyler wandered the halls of his hectic school. Mingle the chaos: the slamming of locker doors and the whispers of countless memories. Every step seemed to tread not only upon linoleum floors but through the years spent inside these walls, with graduation hanging on the horizon—ominous and distant—just like some dark storm. His heart was a mosaic of joy, sorrow, and unsaid dreams, each tile in the image a memory of triumphed hurdles and friendships made on the journey and the inevitable farewells that left permanent marks on his soul. Tyler could not help but think of Quinn, the friend who vanished like a sudden wisp of smoke at the beginning of his high school years.

With Quinn leaving, a line in the sand had been established in Tyler's life. In doing so, he and Kyle became an inseparable duo left to weather grief and growth. Their shared loss had deepened when Quinn's once contagious laughter went out of the world of the living by a cruel twist of fate one summer. Forever unbreakable, beacons of light in each other's lives, a bond between Tyler and Kyle. Yet in the whispering memories, remembering the things that used to be, Tyler felt his reality creep back. Why had Kyle gone quiet?

Lost in thought, Tyler nearly plowed into a figure that stepped out from around the corner: Kyle. "Ky, you—you look different," Tyler stammered, his voice a blend of awe and uncertainty before him, a transformed version of the friend he'd known. Kyle looked different and even more self-assured in a way that Tyler could not pinpoint, but it wasn't just a matter of his confidence. Dangling around his neck was a striking, gold chain link necklace; it absorbed the light in the hall and seemed to reflect with a glowing illumination. The crosshatching of gold did little to cover the emerald, green jewel it encased, "where have you been?" Tyler said, looking at the jewel—an out-of-place accessory for Kyle, but it did fit him in a way Tyler didn't understand. Something material seemed to embody a change that had not yet reached him internally.

"Yeah, and you look different, too," Kyle finally answered as they appraised each other, his eyes landing on the silver band around Tyler's finger. The unvoiced questions between them quickly became deafening, a void expanding into every second of the run-in. It was a momentary distraction, and the question still dangled from Tyler's mind: where had Kyle been? "I'll fill you in after classes," Kyle finally replied as the final bell tolled, marking the beginning of another school day. Tyler had never seen Kyle so evasive. They both went their separate ways, and Tyler was now among the hustle of students, feeling way more anxious than before the encounter with Kyle.

He turned to see the busy hall where Kyle had disappeared into the nearby restroom. Tyler considered waiting for him in the hall and ditching his class but resisted the urge. He made himself go on and walk to his first class of the day. The room was already flickering with shadows of the projector—typical when there was a substitute.

Tyler entered the dark classroom and sat, reading the teacher's instructions before taking notes about the video. But soon, time seemed to stretch into eternity, leaving Tyler adrift again in a sea of thoughts as his focus was shattered by the weight of the ring on his finger and the royal lineage it was supposed to represent. What would his life be like if he believed in the invisible thrown? His eyes came to rest on the incomplete scribbles of his notepad, reaching for a strand of motivation to finish his work. But another sound in the darkness ensnared Tyler's attention—a voice from the edge of memory was speaking, echoing, it seemed, with the kind of familiarity that could freeze his blood on a dime. The same voice he had heard in that place between consciousness and oblivion as he awakened at Scotler Manor.

Man 1: Alexos…

The noise made his head jerk, only to discover the room silent—the effect contagious. Multiple students dozed off or slumped over their desks in the classroom, fast asleep. While others were wide awake, their faces glowing, smaller screens in their palms entertaining them. Tyler shook the memory of the voice, stretching above himself, trying to reawaken his bones. He sat upright, attention returning, but the faint whisper returned. This time louder than the first, the world around Tyler started to dissolve, leaving him to hang in nothingness, light, and darkness, dancing in a timeless embrace as his breath escaped him while the voice continued.

Man 1: Alexos…Alexos…

The ring on his finger pulsed with a life of its own, coursing through his body in shockwaves that surged through his veins. Tyler threw his head back as they overcame him. His world spun as the voice grew louder, taking form in the whirls of vibrant hues weaving through the darkness like delicate strands of silk. These wisps were colored with the intensity of the voice. The louder it became, the more the tentacles brightened and surged forward in full power.

The very air itself was painted with its commanding tone. Images began to take shape in them—flashes of Kyle in some ancient place, the emerald jewel given to him, and then his pain and fear. The emotions were palpable to Tyler, suffocating him, until finally, as swiftly as the vision and voice had come, everything shattered, throwing Tyler back into the stark reality of the quiet classroom—his heart racing, his breath a ragged echo of what he had just endured. The classroom remained unchanged. His classmates were unaware of the odyssey he had just crossed in one heartbeat.

For Tyler, though, the world would never look the same again. The ring, the voice, the ancient knowledge paved before him, the unspoken truth between him and Kyle—all of it had set him upon a course with no turning back, and that much was evident now—"Alexos," he said to himself. What did it mean, and how did it involve the always-ordinary Kyle?

*

Tyler was determined more than ever to get some answers from Kyle. The vision and the voice in his head were so vivid, but what did they mean? Tyler looked down at the clock on his phone again as he waited in the football field's bleachers. It had been nearly two hours since classes ended, and the school grounds had fallen silent. Only a few lingering extracurricular students remain. Tyler sent a third text message to Kyle, asking where he was and pleading that they talk, but there was still no response.

****

CHAPTER ELEVEN
THE TIME WOES

Tyler felt a labyrinth of emotions as the days of uneasy silence trickled by—each unanswered message and phone call another layer to the unraveling of Tyler's life. He had never been more divided in his life. His head was spinning constantly from everything happening, unsure where to place his focus: on his suddenly strained friendship with Kyle, the past that called to him, or finding more answers to age-old questions. He felt like he was being swept up by it all and needed to find his clarity. Under normal circumstances, one would have been right on the other's doorstep to smooth things over when the void was getting too deep between them, but these were far from average times. Tyler's life was changing so drastically that he thought maybe it was all for the better that Kyle remained at a safe distance until he had time to figure out just what in the world, he had gotten himself into.

His journey ahead promised no clarity, with each step leading further into the maze. His bedroom had become a cocoon of thoughts as he sat at his desk before an empty notebook page. His finger played along the edge of the table's surface, eyebrows furrowed, considering the infinite possibilities he made up. When suddenly, he heard the creak of his bedroom door. He spun to see Rebecca standing in the doorway.

Her face seemed softened and caring, reminding Tyler of the face she had the day she sent him to summer camp with Kyle and Quinn for the first time. Her lips twitched slightly as if she were rehearsing her words, but before she had a chance to open her mouth, Tyler voiced his earlier thoughts.

"I need to go back to Scotler Manor to see James and the others," he said, his words bursting out of the cocoon shell of the space. They hung heavy in the air as Tyler watched Rebecca's quiet expression. A flash of concern crossed her face as she moved to sit on the edge of his bed. Her voice was cautious.

"I think, maybe, you should take some time to process all of this," she started, "graduation is right around the corner, and it might be better to play it safe for now." He could hear the fear laced through her words as if they barred the very windows and doors of the house out of protective love from a guardian who foresaw the danger that lay in the way of pursuing the truth. At this moment, Tyler let the protectiveness of his aunt's words keep the world at bay as he went into the depths of his mind about the possibility, seeking the courage to embrace the unknown and the wisdom to navigate the uncharted waters in his reality. Despite Rebecca's caution, Tyler returned to his unshaken resolve.

"It's the only way forward for me, for us." He asserted, "Visiting the manor will shed light on what I need to know about my life...our lives." He went on moving beside Rebecca, pulling her close. "Help me make sense of all this and find the truth for myself."

Tears pooled in Rebecca's eyes as she looked at Tyler. After a long breath, she could only give in to Tyler's unbreakable spirit and nodded. "We can go," she murmured, her voice like a gentle breeze that carried the whiff of change.

Soon, Tyler found himself behind the wheel of his car—his car, he was still adjusting to the idea. Though he was not alone, the presence of Rebecca and Rion at his side, his guardians—was a comforting reminder of the family ties that tethered him to the world. Rion insisted Tyler drive, having found his newfound freedom. The trip was a mostly silent covenant as Tyler navigated the winding roads, perhaps aiding his concentration on his driving skills. His surroundings seemed to blur past like fleeting stop-motion pictures until the manor rose before them.

A monument of beauty, even more awe-gazing than Tyler remembered. As Tyler coasted the car to a stop and its engine silenced, Rion's voice suddenly broke the silence. Leaning forward, a twinkle of mischief in his eyes: "Well, Tyler, I must say, for a second there, I thought we were just about to hit the curb," he joked, the warmth of his voice wrapping the words in an affectionate embrace of another one of his jokes. His careless laughter chased away a bit of tension in the air, if not all of it. Rebecca's laughter that followed matched his, and Tyler couldn't help but join in, soothing the edges of his anxiety as they exited the car.

Before them, the manor stood, its doors a gateway to revelations and possible trials. The vast, heavy double doors brought his heart to drumming anticipation. The door swung open, and behind it, Caleb stood with a smile that lit up his whole face, welcoming features all aglow.

"We're all waiting in here," he gestured, stepping aside.

Inside, the dimming light of dusk streamed through large windows, which were screened by window shades. The air inside held a breath of anticipation as Tyler stepped into the foyer; a sense of déjà vu enveloped him. Reminding him of the last visit to the manor. As he entered the large formal space with his guardians, where the Scotler family sat, Tyler saw their faces as Caleb joined them. They appeared as statues to him, intricately placed throughout the room. The fireplace blazed at the opposite end, James and Diana on the long white couch, Kodi at the mantle of the fire, and Caleb in the same chair Tyler sat in his first visit.

The blaze of the fire added a warm glow across the room, illuminating these figures gathered in its embrace. The firelight danced and accentuated their features, their surreal perfection. Diana and the twins seemed to absorb the light, their sun-kissed skin highlighted in golden hues.

A silent interlude stretched between them, the tension building until the quiet was broken by the soft clatter from the kitchen in the next room. A young woman entered with a tray of glasses, which appeared to be chilled water with a lemon peel slice. She went to the center of the room, silently, keeping her gaze low, and placed the tray on the center table before hurrying out of the room again. "Thank you," Diana said softly before the young woman could escape the reach of her voice. Rion and Rebecca seized the moment of broken tension to find their seats.

Rebecca was beside Diana on the couch, and Rion was against the mantle wall, picking up a glass of the cool liquid as he moved into position. There was only one unoccupied space in the room, a second matching armchair beside Caleb. Tyler crossed the room, feeling the attention on him as he sat in the chair. Rebecca reached for a glass of water.

"Why don't you start with your questions, Tyler?"

Tyler's eyes settled on the ring he wore, the symbol of destiny and a burden not entirely his. An obvious question sprung forth in his mind: "Why me? Why was I chosen to bear the weight of all this?" His words started flowing out of him like a gushing fountain, his eyes not leaving the ring until the fountain's waters ran dry. He finally lifted his head and watched the others exchange silent glances. James finally spoke.

"Unfortunately, everyone in this room has limited knowledge of why things are how they are. We have only been told what secrets the royal family chose to share—the rest was kept until they met their end—surely even after that." He replied solemnly, a clear combination of regret and actual unknowing, "Kodi, would you bring the book from the study here for Tyler?" Kodi nodded slowly, although his steps toward the staircase were slow, brows just slightly drawn up, lips in a thin line—a silent refusal of the task and a hint of reluctance, maybe. Tyler briefly considered whether Kodi or

Caleb would have wished to be the chosen ones.

Why hadn't they been anyway? A few seconds later, Kodi returned, giving Tyler the book. "We know this book and the ring you wear now were meant for those of royal descent. Without one or the other, and the blood that runs in your veins, these secrets, the ones we do not know, would be lost to us all." James said, leaning forward from the couch, "some of the pages in this book tell us something of the past, while others are blank as you have seen. Though," he turned to glance at the others in the room again before returning to Tyler, "Though, I suspect now that you have these things in your possession, more will be revealed."

Tyler tapped his fingers against the book's fragile pages as he spoke, careful of its delicate, time-worn pages. "So, this book is some kind of magic journal?" The question seemed to hang there with the magnitude of his role. He looked up at the unsure expressions in the room.

"Perhaps," Diana replied.

"Some have said the journals crafted by the royals connect to the ancestors or even the greater cosmos itself," James added. Though, his voice was fleeting like shadows at dusk.

"Your mother used to say when she wrote in and read from the journals, it was as if her subconscious was speaking to her," Rebecca said in a low, earnest tone.

Tyler's mind was beginning to blur again, "So I need to discover all of this on my own then," his voice was soiled in sadness, "just answer this: if you know who and where the Cerif is, why haven't you stopped them yourselves and take back this kingdom?" Tyler hadn't realized the gravity of his statement as the air in the room grew still. Then, he conceived a new idea: staying amongst the echoes of the ancient knowledge offered by the worn pages he held at Scotler Manor was his best bet. If those who claimed to protect him couldn't—or wouldn't tell him the answers he sought, he would unravel the ball of yarn himself. Rebecca's eyes peered into him as if recognizing the anguish boiling within Tyler's very being.

"I want to stay with the Scotlers and figure this out." The words formed and spewed into existence faster than Tyler could control before Rebecca could answer. They offered him not just protection but opportunity. It was an opportunity to delve into the journal's secrets, understand the essence of his royal bloodline, and confront the shadows that lurked within its pages. The opportunity to forge his path, discover the strength within, and face the question that haunts this destiny's very foundation: How does one reclaim a kingdom lost to darkness?

"Tyler," Rebecca started.

"I think it's a good idea," Caleb added. His words caught Tyler off guard, stealing his focus. He looked over at Caleb with a curious and grateful expression for the support, and, with his nod, an unspoken feeling of security rippled between them.

"Rebecca? Rion? We are fine with it," Diana added.

Tyler saw the faces of the room as a cautious glance passed between Rebecca and Rion, who gave a slight nod of approval. Rebecca turned toward him, meeting his gaze, and brought the cooled liquid to her lips one last time before sitting it on the table.

"We can all stay for the weekend."

*

Later that night, Tyler found his way back to the same room that had welcomed him on his first visit to Scotler Manor: the guest room, heavy with moonlight. Rebecca and Rion were a whisper away down the hall. In its full glory, the moon shone through the expansive windows that stretched from floor to ceiling, bathing the room in ethereal light. The only inorganic light came from a single lamp perched on the small desk wedged into the corner of the room. It was dim enough to quiet the vastness of the night beyond the window. Tyler's eyes kept wandering back to the journal sitting open before him, his previous encounter with it at the forefront of his psyche.

Despite the fear pricking his side—he submerged back into the pages anyway, trying to draw out some form of order from the chaos. His fingers traced the pages of the journal over ink blots that danced over the spread, across textures of wrinkles and tears that spoke to its age and wear. As he flipped beyond the familiar text, blank pages stared back, a silent challenge. He rifled through them, spurred by hope in James's cryptic assurances that secrets would be revealed to the royal bloodline, until a solitary ink blot at the corner of a page stopped him. It morphed before his eyes, foreign symbols at first that coalesced into a single line:

Twice, in time, twofold align. Bled blood combine.

Tyler breathed the words, which launched a waterfall of sensations mirroring his feelings that day in class. The inked words vanished almost as quickly as they appeared. For a moment, the room was still. Then, suddenly, the room's tranquility was shattered as shadows descended. Darkness poured in, swarming in again, filling his sight with an ocean of black. Tyler was thrown into a vortex of visions—faces flickered in his periphery, the familiar voice returning in distortion. The whispers crescendoed to a symphony of unintelligible fervor. The abrupt entrance of James into the room broke the communication, and the darkness seemed to shrink away at his appearance like scalded flesh. The ring on Tyler's finger burst into light, driving away the remaining dark and leaving Tyler on his knees, gasping to catch his breath as he watched his world dissolve into chaos before his eyes. "What was—" He exclaimed, in fear and amazement.

"The darkness was here. We felt it," James replied, rushing from the room, Tyler at his heels, "an entity from centuries ago. We do not know exactly." The rest was a blur, and not far behind, Diana and the twins followed, each of their faces etched with worry. James combed through the bookshelves. "The ring does more than unlock secrets—it protects you from the dangerous ones," As the implications of the warning and what James had said bore down on him, Tyler's only solace was found in an armchair in the study.

"James, there was something in the book, a line of text," Tyler flipped through the pages of the journal. It said something about bled blood combining…"

"A message?" Diana asked.

"What does it mean?" Tyler asked.

"I do not know. It could very well be the deception of the True Vampires." James replied, "The Cerif, do not want to see the return of the royal bloodline. A group of trueborn vampires, not turned, but descendants of the first vampires—

they see themselves as true royals, though they are not." The idea of vampires still stained Tyler's mind, filling it with the lore of television depictions: coffins in unkept castles, cold diamond-like skin, and stakes to the heart.

"Vampires…overthrowing my royal ancestors…"

Tyler said.

"True Vampires are very dangerous beings. The Cerif grew too powerful and betrayed the royal family," Rebecca said as she came in with Rion. Scotler Manor was no longer a haven for revealing the truths of the past but rather a battle-ground where the echoes met the uncertainty of the future— with Tyler at the heart of it all.

"You connected with the past tonight, Tyler."

James added.

CHAPTER TWELVE

THE REIGNING ROYAL

The weekend was running together, the world around them a far-off memory as Tyler and James sorted through page after page of books that towered above them. "How do you have all of this history on the royal family?" Tyler asked.

"The Shafeir are the trusted guards of the royal family. What was reclaimed of history was divided and hidden, protected from the Cerif after the kingdom fell." James climbed the ladder against the bookshelf, reaching for archives.

"There are more Shafeir?" Tyler looked up the ladder. His arms were filled with a stack of books and journals, thin with rounded edges, others thick and square, some encased in aged leather. "Did you find all of these at auction houses?" At that moment, Tyler realized he had not brought up the article he had found online since meeting the Scotlers. The question called for James to stop midway down the ladder and place yet another book onto the growing stack in Tyler's arms.

"Yes, there are other Shafeir, very few, scattered across the ether. As for the book, the journal was the only one hidden amongst the mortals here—for good reason." James replied.

"Because it's magic," Tyler added, his voice still toying with the nearly impossible idea. "I still don't quite understand all of this. Vampires, hybrids, and—what exactly am I again, Vasi—" The word still got caught up in his throat.

"Vasi-li-kos," James annunciated, "or simply Vasili. The journal will reveal more to you in time." Tyler followed him as he spoke to the wooden desk, placing the stack of books in his arms on its edge. He considered stopping to question why James deferred to the journal so much when he probed into the answers he was given rather than tell him what he knew. The cryptic pages of the journal appeared to be just as dangerous as the True Vampires James spoke of. However, a voice broke into the study before Tyler could follow up.

"James? Tyler? Are you up here?" Rebecca crept into the room. "Kodi said I might find you two up here." She continued to move through the room until they met in an embrace. Tyler smiled, realizing his subconscious yearned for it. "We're so glad to be here with you," she said.

"Where is Uncle Rion, anyway?" Tyler asked, pulling back, their gaze on each other.

"I told him it was probably best he returned to work." A flash of confusion passed over Tyler's face as Rebecca spoke, "he loves you, we both do, but he has little connection to this world we're a part of." It was true—as Tyler thought in silence for a moment, he agreed with the notion. His uncle did marry into the family, but also, in the moment, he felt a sliver of envy arise, the option to retreat to normalcy all alluring—an option that appeared not to exist for him. He nodded, a silent agreement to the decision.

"Rebecca, please join us," James interjected.

"What are you two hoping to find in all these books?" She asked as she shifted a few books off an armchair to sit.

A question Tyler was beginning to ask himself after days of skimming so many pages. In this quest for answers, his mind frequently drifted to the one person he knew to be a treasure trove of knowledge—his best friend, Kyle. More and more, their weakening bond was starting to fuel a growing spite.

"Since Tyler read from the journal, we have been searching for more ancient Vasili language. Perhaps you can help."

She breathed heavily and pushed herself off the armchair with her hands, slicing the air in a gesture of uncertainty. "I can try," she said, skepticism in her voice. "The royal family adopted me, and Alina ensured I was treated as such. But truly, I'm no royal." She approached the desk and picked up an open book. The room became a silent search again. Tyler opened the journal given to him again, flipping its pages.

As he returned to the blank section, where he saw the fading message, another ink blot appeared. "I may have found something; the ink appeared again," Tyler said.

"It may be another message. Focus this time, Tyler." James urged, "Do not let it overtake you; the ring will ground you to this reality." He appeared by Tyler's side with Rebecca.

"I don't see anything," Rebecca said, running her fingers along the journal's edge.

"Only to be read by royal blood," James replied. Tyler watched as the ink swirled, scrambling foreign symbols again before coming into view. He heeded James's words, allowing the returning sensation from the ring to ground him. The ring on his finger had a throbbing heartbeat as it began to glow.

"It says, *Twelve, of twelve, nine. Midnights eve divine.*"

"Twelve of twelve nine…" James repeated, rushing to the wooden desk again. Tyler shut the book, severing the connection and sensation of the ring before it overtook him. The message was unclear to him at first, but then suddenly, an idea—a long shot idea worth attending to if it meant more answers. Tyler joined James at the desk as he scribed on a scrap of paper. Grabbing a pen of his own, he added to the text. "Does this mean anything?"

Twice, in time, twofold align.
Bled blood combine. Twelve, of
twelve, nine. Midnights eve divine.

Tyler watched his aunt's and James's faces for a long moment. Until Rebecca shifted, her brows raised in realization. It was the pivotal moment the trio needed. "Of course, the Connected Key," she said, intrigue trailing her words.

"How did you figure this out, Tyler?" James asked.

"The other night, when I read the journal, I saw the first part of the phrase."

James paced the floor, deep in thought, staring out of the large window, a hand to his chin. "Not deception, a key, direction," he murmured, "I believe you are right, Rebecca. This refers to the Connected Key."

"What's a Connected Key?" Tyler asked.

The study doors were thrust open with alarming force as soon as the words left his lips. Diana and the twins were entering, Diana's face a mask of urgent distress. "Something's wrong," she blurted out, her eyes wild with fear.

"What is it, Diana?" James asked.

"I've had a vision—our location, it's been compromised. The Cerif knows where we are, as revealed by Tyler's connection with the journal." Full of thought, the room was filled with strangled strategy. Rebecca inched closer to Tyler, arms draped around his shoulders in an act of protection. The weight of impending peril seemed to squeeze the walls closer on Tyler.

His heart, beating madly in his chest, echoed from his frayed nerves. Just moments before, he had felt the stirrings of control, a semblance of direction in this labyrinth. Now, this short-lived sense of empowerment had flown from him, replaced by an old enemy: uncertainty and danger.

"It is time we made our preparations," James replied.

***

It was a heavy revelation—a diabolic cloud of unsaid words. Tyler's mind ran a hundred miles an hour, piecing fragments together: his connection to the journal and family legacy. Even as Diana's dire warning waned, Tyler was frozen beside Rebecca on the white sofa in the front room of the or-ganized chaos at Scotler Manor. Diana orchestrated the plan as she and the twins unfurled oversized maps across the center table, plotting their travel.

"The Cerif have allies in this realm searching for the Connected Key." She glanced over to Tyler and pointed at a spot on the map, "if we travel here, we may be able to intercept one and gain information about their plans."

"Jakob in Venice?" Caleb asked.

Diana nodded, "he may still be in Greece, however. He will help us or try to kill us." The gravity of the situation anchored Tyler to his spot on the couch. He watched as the twins took Diana's direction. James came from another room carrying suitcases.

"When will you leave?" He asked sitting the cases down.

"Kodi, will you come with me?" Diana asked, her voice reluctant as if she were asking the impossible of him. Kodi and Caleb exchanged glances, the silence in the room pulling Tyler from his stasis. He recalled a brief talk about the twins' connection with James and reading about their unique bonds in ancient texts—the idea fascinated him.

"It's a bit more than twinship," Diana said as if responding to Tyler's thoughts. "The twins were born from the blood of the royal Vasilikos, as all Shafeir were. They are most powerful and connected when they are together."

*

The sun started to dip, the windows smeared with amber light and warmth. A certain level of comfort came to Tyler from sitting on the cool floor of his guest quarters. Though it was inconsistent with the turmoil inside him. It was a welcomed moment. The sun's rays pierced the thick cloud coverage that plagued the town for months. Tyler was tired, fatigue clinging to him like another skin, resulting from the mental marathon he was thrust into.

The news of the Cerif finding his location and his still unforeseen responsibilities and expectations as a royal were each a wave crashing over him after another. All of this had been unknown to Tyler only a few weeks ago. The reality haunted him despite his reluctance to follow the path before him. His search for the truth turned into something very different from what he had expected. Tyler did not want to disappoint his late parents or those surrounding him now. A desire pressing heavily on his conscience. His trust in Rebecca and increasing confidence in the Scotler family offered him a glimmer of hope in the troubled sea of his thoughts.

He desired the truth so terribly, with a resolve so fragile as it was fierce, he committed to giving his all in the unfolding narrative of his fate—discovering the truth at all costs. Vulnerable and alone in the room, Tyler reached for his phone, seeking a lifeline in Kyle one more time as if somehow that gesture could return him to a place of normalcy within the gathering storm. However, he found no response to his messages, further isolating him from what was.

CHAPTER THIRTEEN
THE YESTERYEARS

The waning hours of the weekend sat Tyler at a crossroads in Scotler Manor. The return to high school loomed an unavoidable event: A place he would otherwise be happy to return to had life been what it once was—reunited with Kyle, but his recent absence and silence had sown seeds of frustration and anger in Tyler's heart. Even so, there was still the undeniable urge to escape it, not let his trouble with Kyle or school disrupt the truths he was to unlock within the manor's walls. Tyler walked the long corridor from his guest room to the kitchen. It seemed like the newly constructed walls themselves were heavy with the overbearing of secrets.

Descending the staircase, he found Rebecca sitting alone in the kitchen, seated at the stone slab dining table with a glass in her hand. Its contents were all too familiar to him: red liquid.

"Rebecca," he started, approaching the table. She turned to face him, eyes heavy in euphoria as if she were drunk at merely the sight of the red liquid, "about school…"

Tyler trailed off with a reluctant heart.

"If you aren't ready to go back, I understand. Take a few more days if you need, honey." It was the reprieve Tyler needed from the imminent return to academia. His plea had not been so much for time but for solace, away from the wedge that now seemed to separate him from Kyle. The manor, journal, and ancient books were reason enough for him to stay awhile longer. He left Rebecca to her indulgence and returned to the small desk in his guest quarters with the ancient journal, seeking further answers from its pages.

From memory, he sketched the odd moment in his head from his classroom: the unexplained vision of the supernatural, the vividness of the voice, unfamiliar to him, echoing in the background. The singular word it whispered was almost a directive or an idea. He said that word aloud again, "Alexos," setting the room to move as it slipped from his lips, the journal too reacting, coming alive in front of him. The pages fluttered as if the wind had taken hold of them, and the ink blots started to form, moving, combining in new symbols, then words, a story unwinding to speak to him.

THE STORY OF ALYX THE GREAT

Early in conception, suspicion sparked—an anomaly among the royal bloodline, the birth blood marked. Twins. Gemini born—twice blessed by the ancient thorn, more royal, more powerful than forebearers born. Yes, that was when the discovery was adorned.

Tyler watched as the words poured as if drawn from a hollow container onto the page.

Such raw power cannot be contained or controlled. Bringing even the royals before the untold, death of the Gemini would be a mercy, though the ancestors held no will to curse thee. It was the ancient one, older than time—the mother, the creator, such an act of the divine—birth of another, the first of his kind. A gift from the originals, Alyx the Great, his name through time.

Imbued with stone, emerald, and gold in tone—the protector, and guide, of the twins in tide. Prokìmos O Alexos— the oath taken in stride. Wives in three, the Great bestowed blood and curse to many.

Now is the task through the tree, to the chosen protector of the Connected Key.

As Tyler read and reread the words on the page, the expected overwhelming force never came. There was no overbearing presence, nor did the ring on his finger take on the same throbbing or light. Something grounded him in place: a quiet certainty that he was connected to the book, allowing him to see its secrets. Once the story ends, a sort of epiphany lights within—the emerald green jewel in the tale matches the description of the one he saw around Kyle's neck. The discovery propels him. The moment of truth had come to bridge the ever-increasing gap between him and Kyle.

There was something more going on with him. Tyler exits the room on a mission to confront his friend when the sudden encounter with the Scotler twins in the hallway unexpectedly delays him. "Woah, look out," Kodi said as Tyler bumped into him, journal in hand. Tyler looked up at the twins, his mind tangled in a web of thoughts hardly recognizing the figures ahead of him. The sight of them was a blunt reminder of their mirrored image in every conceivable way, from the arch of their curious brows to the identical tilt of their heads.

"Where are you headed, Tyler?" Caleb asked. There was a brief pause, a suspended moment in time where curiosity danced in the air between them.

"The book, there was something about an amulet and a protector. I need to find Kyle."

Tyler stammered over his words, finding the memory through the web of his thoughts. Recognition flickered in the pairs of eyes before him, accompanied by a shared glance. A clear sign they knew something Tyler did not. His attention shifted, drawn to the twins' evasive demeanor. "What is it?" Tyler urged.

Met with silence, it quickly strengthened Tyler's resolve to draw the answers out of the elusive sources at the manor. Peering down the long corridor, he turned toward the open door leading into the study. The voices met him at a distance. Within moments, Tyler was at the open door, stepping into the study, where James, Rebecca, Diana, and Rion were found, their hushed tones growing silent at his presence while the twins trailed after Tyler's footsteps. "You've all been promising me answers, but all I have are more questions," he said, this time with a tone hardened by frustration. "What is this Connected Key?"

With his sharp announcement, there was a shift in the room. Rebecca lowered her gaze, a flicker of distress betraying her composed composure; her fingers twitched against the fabric of her shirt. Beside her, Rion sat stiffly—jaw clenched, face stoic—as the question lay heavy in the air. Rion's eyes seemed to focus on some indistinct point in the room. Tyler thought it might be an answer or a way out from this horrible truth hanging between them. James exhaled a nearly inaudible sigh and dropped his shoulders a bit. The tension felt in the room reflected what Tyler was struggling with within.

However, it was Diana who kept Tyler's eye contact, her demeanor calm and contained with an unblinking, fixed look.

Her deep brown eyes were hypnotizingly still, sympathetic and mournful. It almost seemed like she knew what was going on far more than the others. She didn't speak but rose from her chair, moving up to Tyler until she was right in front of him. Tyler prepared himself for yet another unraveling of a thread he so desperately tugged at. "The first Connected Key was an anomaly in the bloodline, a pair of twins," her voice was low, comforting, and truthful.

Tyler was sure of that. She spoke of the same story the journal told him only moments ago. Rebecca stood abruptly in objection as Diana trailed off.

"Diana," she started, cautioning, "we should wait to explain all of this." Tyler was confused by this, but his uncle Rion followed suit and stood before he could protest.

"Rebecca, the time for secrets is behind us…" he said, his voice only a whisper.

"Twins have a deep connection; Tyler should know why he's felt this way."

Kodi chimed in, hinting that Tyler was on the cusp of discovering a similar connection. Overwhelmed and confused by a mélange of cryptic exchanges and elusive truths, Tyler stood amidst the room, his mind a whirlwind of bewilderment from Diana's words. "Much like the other royal Vasili, the Connected Key draws from ancient power—the difference is what their uniqueness allows the power to become since it is a direct connection to The Source. Making the twins the most powerful beings in the realm—their limits quite unknown to anyone." Diana's voice turned cryptic as she continued, "The Connected Key is essential to the survival and reign of the royals."

"But what do protectors have to do with all of this?" Tyler asked, impatient for further clarification. His mind lingering on the connection between the enigmatic amulet and his best friend, James, stepped forward, joining Diana.

"The Alexos are bound by oath to protect the Connected Key and were given an amulet to do so." The revelation was as startling as it was perplexing to Tyler.

"It's true, Ty."

A voice broke into the room, familiar and foreign to Tyler's ears. He spun to the study's door to see Kyle standing beside the Scotler twins. The charged atmosphere was the catalyst that shattered Tyler's remaining composure. The realization that his confidant, the person he considered a pillar of his normal life, was intricately woven into the fabric of his new reality left him beyond all comprehension. Betrayal and secrecy sliced through him, severing the last strands of trust of anyone in the room as he grappled with the reality thrown at his feet. Kyle was not an ally but a keeper of secrets and a guardian bound by an oath.

Tyler's body went numb, and the room fell silent as the pieces continued to come together in Tyler's mind, sinking into the very air around him. Kyle's voice was a distant, inaudible noise, but Tyler assumed he asked for the room as its occupants began filing out, leaving him and Kyle alone. Tyler's eyes searched for anything to focus on as if waiting for a reasonable answer to befall him suddenly. He felt his throat constrict and his mouth run dry.

"Breathe, Ty," Kyle said, his voice closer.

Was breathing an option? Tyler wasn't sure he remembered how; it was all a blow to the gut. The truth still reverberating in the inner of his ears. Tyler finally slumped into a chair, the weight of reality pressing down like a physical force. Kyle knelt in front of him. Though he was part of the chaos, his presence still held some strange comfort, a refuge that seemed to seep into the cracks of Tyler's fractured mind.

The next few minutes were a blur. Tyler didn't remember how or when they left the study, but his surroundings shifted, his back suddenly against the edge of the bed in his guest room. But Kyle was still in front of him. Not a word passed between them. The room felt simultaneously confining and expansive. Tyler shifted to the floor further, the coolness of its surface now against his back in a calming sensation as he gazed at the ceiling. Kyle eventually joined him, "Oh, you were right. The floors in this house are oddly comfortable." Kyle's voice finally broke the silence.

"Told you," Tyler said in a dry reply as they lay opposite of one another. Kyle momentarily propped himself up on an elbow and met Tyler's silent gaze. Tyler caught a moment's glimpse of something in his eyes—a depth of emotion: sorrow, regret, pain, or perhaps affection? It was as if an unseen hand had peeled back a layer Tyler hadn't seen before, revealing a torrent of unspoken feelings beneath the surface.

For a moment, Tyler toyed with the idea that there possibly was something more, but the enormity of the revelations left no room for such considerations. With a slight nod, Kyle returned to the floor beside him, and the two continued in silence—adrift in a sea of their tumultuous thoughts, yet strangely anchored by the presence of each other. "Where were you all this time, Ky? Why show up now?" Tyler asked, his throat finding the hydration it desperately needed.

"I thought taking the oath was going to be a breeze. Turns out it's not such an easy process. I was planning on finding you at school, but after I found out you hadn't been there, I knew I had to come here," Kyle paused.

"What was it like? The oath." Tyler asked.

"Honestly, it was scary as hell. My mom took me to this old underground family crypt and gave me this amulet—the same one my dad wore. Remembering him at that moment almost made me reconsider. It supposedly grants its wielder some power," Kyle replied.

"What did you have to do?" Tyler asked.

"My mom, she read from an old book down there, and then I had to use a blade and cut my hand," Kyle lifted his hand above them, but there was no visible wound Tyler could see. "It healed freakishly fast after the oath was done. I guess it must be this jewel made from green Chinese jade." Tyler cocked his head to see the gold chain around Kyle's neck, the stone encased in gold in his hand. "My dad was sworn to be the next protector of the Connected Key, but the Cerif made sure that wouldn't happen." Kyle continued a spark of anger in his voice.

"So, that's why you never talked about your dad?" Tyler asked. His question met with a silent nod. Tyler was beginning to understand Kyle more. "We've both been given high expectations to live up to, with you being a sworn protector and me—" The subsiding details suddenly flooded back as Tyler spoke. "Twins?" he whispered, sitting up suddenly.

"What is it?" Kyle asked, springing up.

The blur of time happened again. Tyler stood at the grand staircase, listening to the voices below. He and Kyle descended the steps to find the others in the front room. "It's lovely to see you again, Patricia," James said as Tyler and Kyle entered the room.

"Mom?" Kyle said, approaching the woman. It had been so long since Tyler had seen her that he had nearly forgotten what Patricia looked like. Her copper skin, short hair, and calm disposition. She embraced Kyle before turning her gaze to Tyler.

"Tyler," she said in a soft voice.

"Mrs. Huntington," he replied, stepping into her embrace. Surprised, he could manage a slight smile. "You all know each other?" Tyler followed up.

"Yes. We knew Kyle's father, Derek Alix Huntington," James replied, exchanging glances with Diana and Rebecca. Tyler saw sorrow in the faces around the room, which carried heavy remorse guilt, and fear should Kyle meet the same grim fate his father did.

"Is your brother Rennon here as well, then?" Patricia asked, withdrawing from their embrace to meet Tyler's gaze as he wrestled with the thought of Kyle's future. Her words stirred more than she realized in Tyler—the whirlwind of emotions returning to him in a flood. Rennon? Was that his name? The mystery whose existence was only a possibility to him not long ago.

The expression on Patricia's face meant she read the depths of confusion and questioning Tyler had. Her expression shifted to dread as she realized she just spoiled the news. Tyler looked past her at James and Rebecca with something beyond anger in his voice, confronting the idea.

"Where is he?"

*

The moments of silence felt like hours, then days, as Tyler's question hung in the air. "I'm sorry, I just assumed," Patricia started, spinning to James and the others with an apologetic hand to her mouth. Kyle ushered her to a seat as Tyler approached the gob-smacked faces he once could trust.

"It's not your fault. Mrs. Huntington, James, and Rebecca were just about to tell me," Tyler said, a tumultuous mix of anger nearing the cliff's edge of rage.

"You've been separated your entire lives. It was your parent's wish to keep you separated for your safety and the safety of the royal bloodline," Rebecca's voice was full of regret and sadness, carried on her face. Tyler was filled with emotion and questions. They cycled through his mind a bit worriedly. What was his brother like? Did they resemble each other? Where had he been all this time?

As frustration piled on to Tyler, he suddenly felt relief at the thought of a brother washing over him. It kindled a blaze of inquiry in him to believe that maybe he wasn't alone after all. He pictured the kind of relationship they would've had over all these years—perhaps the kind the Scotler twins shared. Slowly, the feeling of comfort dawned on him as the moments flew by. The realization that he would not have to face the burdens assigned to him alone—that someone bound by blood to him would share in them.

*

All the earnest pleas of his aunt, uncle, and even the Scotler twins could not sway Tyler's resolve to leave the manor. There was nothing they could say to him or do for him. Betrayal and discontent eroded Tyler's trust into the walls surrounding him. He felt he was a stranger among those he once called family. As he shoved what clothing he had brought into the manor into a bag, Kyle entered the room. "Ty, you're not doing this alone. I swore to protect you and intend to keep that promise." Tyler hesitated, but he knew Kyle was right. His duty and loyalty were clear.

"Fine," Tyler replied sharply, his back to him.

There was only one place Tyler could think of to escape, a remote campsite up the canyon, away from town. "What are you going to do, Ty?" Kyle asked.

"Go up the canyon. I have no idea after that."

"Maybe it's time you searched for your brother," Kyle said.

"Let's make a pact," Tyler proposed, ignoring the suggestion, his voice steady despite the uncertainty that lay ahead. He spun to face Kyle, "No matter what happens, we'll always stand by each other."

Kyle nodded. Tyler's actions were cemented in place when he and Kyle were out of the manor. "What if the Cerif finds you?" Rebecca pleaded again, the others by her side at the threshold of the manor, as Tyler and Kyle put their bags inside Kyle's car. Tyler met her question with silence as he swung open the passenger door.

"We'll keep in contact." He shouted in reply. Inside the car, Rebecca's question lingered. "What if she's right? What if they find us?" Tyler asked.

"First, I'm driving, so let's see them try to catch us. Second, I have this now." Kyle held the amulet dangling from his neck up. "The odds are not in their favor, mathematically speaking." With a heavy heart, Tyler watched out of his window as Scotler Manor, its occupants, and the lavish gift of a car parked out front became a distant memory out of view.

PART III

CHAPTER FOURTEEN

ENTER SHADOW FOES

With the sun retreating to the shadows, everything around became cool, similar to the mornings Tyler loved when going out for his morning runs. He sat in the passenger side of Kyle's car, watching the countless drops of rain as they danced a silent ballet on the window in rhythmic patterns, a soothing backdrop to his thoughts. Inside, the car was a blanket of warmth, their breathing steaming the glass, forming temporary art that vanished as swiftly as it appeared, only to be reborn with each exhale. Outside, the scenery morphed with every passing mile: trees and landscape blurred into one watercolor blotch through the rain-speckled window. It was as if the world outside mirrored the storm of emotions brewing in Tyler's heart, each droplet reflecting a fragment of his burgeoning curiosity about this brother.

He envisioned what it would be like to share a conversation, hear laughter that carried the same timbre as his own, and exchange thoughts on the trivial and the profound. With each mile he and Kyle passed, Tyler felt like layers of long-secret truths about his family, and himself were finally peeled back. The image of a twin brother, a mirror image of his very being, much like the Scotler twins but a stranger—sparking a constellation of questions and what-ifs. The drive had been an hour long already.

The view out of the window, moving from what was familiar to the unknown, is representative of Tyler's move from the unknown confinements of his life to the uncharted territories of family secrets, newfound connections, and destiny. The rain seemed to part for the car as it sliced through it. Even with the decision to run away from his troubles, Tyler felt the strange, unexplainable pulling to the mysteries that awaited him—a pull toward embracing the truths of the new world he found himself in. It was a world that has always been there, veiled in plain sight, waiting only for the right moment to unveil itself. "Still another hour away," Kyle said, gripping the steering wheel.

"Feels like forever since we had a normal day," Tyler replied, still fixed on the window. As they wound their way up the sinuous road to Crescent Peak—a lookout rumored about among their classmates—the sky gave up its final bits of light, conceding to an impenetrable darkness. The weather, as if coordinating with their ascent, began to grow ferocious: the air thickened with a heavy mist. Like ghostly tendrils, fog crept in from the mountainside, draping the landscape in its gray shroud as the rain picked up to an immediate downpour. Tyler felt the change in the atmosphere, sitting forward in his seat, eyes squinting as he looked through the darkening windshield.

"The weather's turned fast. Ky, the headlights, they're too bright. Is that something up ahead?" He said, pointing at a barely discernible dark figure in the distance. There, standing right in their way, was an indistinct, wavering figure resembling some wild creature or human form. Kyle fumbled a moment with the switch of the headlights before they went out. Tempered by curiosity, he slowed to coast with the car's tires crunching softly in the dampened street and pulled over to a stop.

Kyle tapped the horn—sharply, hopefully, a few blasts to startle the presence into motion. Yet the figure sat as if paralyzed and not of their world, bound in place. The rain fell harder and drummed against the car with unrelenting fury, as if a thousand drummers hammered their beats upon the metal and glass. Visibility dwindled to mere shadows and shapes, and the world outside was reduced to a monochromatic blur of rain and mist. The car's engine was a drowned-out hum against the deluge outside.

Tyler and Kyle exchanged wary glances, their skepticism growing with unease at every second. Who—or what—stood before them, impervious to the storm and their presence? Tyler's eyes adjusted to the darkness, and the figure began taking shape in the downpour. It was a person grounded in their stance on the road ahead as if waiting for something. "Who is that?" Kyle asked. Tyler shook his head slowly, still watching the figure.

"Something isn't right. We need to leave." The feeling sank deep within Tyler as their reality became clear: surrounded by trees, unarmed, and secluded from others—they were alone. "Ky, you don't think it could be one of them, do you?" Tyler asked. His thoughts rushed toward all he learned from James, the library of books, journals, and their discussions. The horrors he read about of ruthless vampire beings were linked to the chilling voices that called to him from the darkness and, most of all, the danger the Cerif posed. Now, without preparation, stood before him an unknown threat. "Kyle, get us out of here."

In an instant, Kyle's instincts took over. His hands flew to the gearshift, executing a swift change, and with another flick, the headlights switched back on while his eyes darted over the seats to the murky road behind them. With a decisive push on the accelerator, the car jerked into reverse, retreating from the ominous figure that loomed ahead. "Hang on!" Kyle shouted as the vehicle picked up speed, its tires screeching in protest against the wet asphalt. Tyler's heart raced, adrenaline surging through his veins as he gripped the armrest, his body tensing in anticipation for what might come next. Tyler's breath became shallow and rapid, but the burst of speed was fleeting.

Gradually, the car slowed as if the night itself were reaching out to stop their escape. The lights flickered, casting eerie shadows on the road as it reluctantly stopped. Leaving them in tense stillness; the only sound the patter of rain against the car and their labored breaths. "What's wrong? Keep going, Ky!" Tyler shouted.

"Trying to! Something's happening to the car." Kyle revved the engine again, and it roared louder the harder he pressed. The wheels screeched and smoked in place, spinning. "Something's holding us back," Kyle yelled in a voice laced with panic. He said determinedly, "If it doesn't let us retreat, then we'll charge forward." Decisively, he grabbed the steering wheel and shifted gears in one swift motion; his hand tightened on the accelerator, releasing the full strength of the engine.

The car raced straight ahead into the figure.

Tyler's heart raced, and he gripped the seat even more as the vehicle surged forward. The world turned into a vortex of shadow and light outside as they ran toward the figure. Its details started to come into sight: a dark-haired woman in black, her figure still amidst all the chaos of the elements. The closer they came, the more her face focused, although it was still fog-covered, making her seem ghostly. Her hair was wet and black, whipping around in the wind as if it were an element of her that was wild and unchained.

Tyler tried to look closer and strained his eyes when a small glimmer shone out at him. She had a weapon. She held a silver blade with an ornate handle, reflecting the sparse light from the car's headlights in menacing flashes.

"Kyle, something is not right," Tyler muttered as the dread tightened its grip and a familiar sensation crept up his neck, a reminder of the visions that plagued him before. That darkness seemed to call out for him. Kyle started to reply when the car's tires suddenly screeched violently. He twisted the steering wheel around in a desperate maneuver as the woman agilely sidestepped. Having drawn her glade, she played a note of terror against the car's metal body, slashing into the back tire. Control slipped away like sand through fingers, the car going into a wild, uncontrollable spin before flipping on its side.

Tyler's world became a dizzying whirl of motion and noise. The motion tossed his body mercilessly, restrained by his seatbelt. Its spinning dance threw him about. In quick flashes, among the disorienting and nauseating spins, he could see the woman's face: a sinister smile spread over her features in the chilling delight of the act. Finally, the wild spinning and scraping stopped and was replaced by a calm hiss of steam and the patter of rain. Pain washed over Tyler like a tidal wave.

Cradling his head, he sought what made it throb so painfully, his thoughts a fog of chaos. Amidst it all, one voice pierced the confusion like a sharp needle to a balloon. Still, Tyler's senses were overwhelmed, teetering on the edge of consciousness, the entire event a nightmare from which he desperately wished to wake.

"Tyler! Tyler, are you okay?!" Kyle called out. Tyler

opened his eyes. With every blink, he tried to clear the disorienting haze from his vision. Then, slowly, his surroundings began forming around him: a grotesque panorama of devastation. And just then, as his vision grew more apparent, out of the wreckage appeared Kyle—his face and arms cut in a network of marks.

The car had become a shattered shell, a crumbled husk, hissing at the rain as it smoked, the sharp tang of burnt metal, and the acrid bite of leaked fluids filling Tyler's nose. Littered through the interior was glass—sparkling like diamonds—glinting harshly in the dim light filtering through the broken windows. Kyle had already escaped the wreckage.

Meanwhile, Tyler dangled in inverted, held only by the seatbelt that saved him. He worked furiously against the belt, fighting the movements with panic and force. With one final tug and struggle to get free from it, he fell from the seat, feeling the wash of relief and the sting of pain. Once free in the open, the cool night air hit him, the rain then just a drizzle as he and Kyle reunited, inspecting the car and the scene.

Tyler braced himself against the ruined sedan, and the

image of the woman on the road returned suddenly and vividly. The danger she posed hung over them like a predator stalking its prey. Tyler's heart was still thumping, his senses on high alert as his eyes traced where the shadowed woman once was on the road. He could almost feel the sense of coming danger raise his senses. "Where is she?" Tyler said, breathless.

Tyler could see the determination in Kyle's face as he, too, scanned the eerie calm that had fallen upon the scene. The rain had let up and left everything around them wet, heavy, and silent. Then, cutting through the stillness, sinister laughter echoed in the distance. Tyler and Kyle gasped in horrified unison and looked back to see the source—the silhouette of the woman, now standing several feet away on the road. "What're we gonna do, Ky?" Tyler's voice quivered with intensifying panic, his fear more tangible than the thick, humid air around them. He pawed through his pockets in a desperate attempt to find his phone and, with a sinking heart, realized it was gone—lost in the upending of their crash. But suddenly, Kyle's body language shifted, changing into an iron-willed determination from the previous apprehension.

"I know what I have to do," Kyle declared. Tyler watched, dumbfounded, as Kyle approached the dark figure, his hand reaching for the amulet he was wearing around his neck. In words Tyler recognized from the cryptic journal, Kyle's voice swelled, resonating with a power that seemed to resonate with the amulet itself.

"*Prokimos O Alexos*," he yelled, and in the next instant, a blinding flash of dazzling green light exploded from the amulet, engulfing Kyle in its splendor. It was so bright that it caused Tyler to shield his eyes with his hand and lurch back simultaneously by the intense power of the energy discharge; his hands met the wet, cold ground to steady him. Peeking through his fingers, Tyler watched with fear and awe as Kyle stood before the dark figure, whose very unearthly power seemed to challenge their reality.

"Kyle!" Tyler's voice snapped, eyes going wide with disbelief. Beneath the moon's light, Kyle began to rise slowly from the wet pavement, his feet lifting off the ground a couple of inches, then a couple of inches more, floating higher and higher into the night sky. Tyler's screams rang out through the cold air, wailing like a tortured banshee as he witnessed the unfathomable transformation unfolding before him. An ethereal light enveloped Kyle, causing his metamorphosis as though it had been cast from the mythical pages of some centuries-old fable.

With a sudden intensity, magnificent, feathered wings burst forth from his back, tearing through his clothes, their expansive span casting imposing shadows on the ground below. The sight was both wondrous and horrific as the light sculpted Kyle's very being, dissolving his clothes and replacing them with gleaming metallic armor that clung to his form like a second skin. Amazed at first, Tyler's initial marvel curdled into dread as he heard Kyle's tortured cries fill the night. "Kyle, stop!" Tyler's plea was frantic, desperate to stop the transformation--but it continued--and when the light faded, and the new form of Kyle was shown, the cries fell silent.

Hovering aloft, Kyle was a figure of mythic proportions, his newly acquired wings gently fanning the air, a glowing sword now clasped in his hand—a weapon that seemed as ethereal as the being who wielded it. Tyler lay motionless on the pavement, his mind grappling with the surreal vision of his transformed friend. The woman's voice cut through the silence again, clear and unnervingly calm. "I know what you are," she said, her voice sent shivers down Tyler's spine.

"I am Aleks—the descendant of Derek Alix, keeper of the Alexos amulet and protector of the Vasilikós and the Connected Key," came a strange voice, resonant and empowered with authority. Tyler's eyes craned up with fear and confusion, looking at the altered figure of his friend—now a stranger—named Aleks. "You have darkness in your heart. Should you continue your pursuit, you will die here," it intoned, its meaning finally clear.

Once more, the woman's laughter rippled in the most chilling way as her gaze fixed on Tyler, slicing the air with the blade. In a flash, she hurtled at him, her every step a promise of impending violence. Panicked, Tyler sprawled backward with his hands, his heart ready to burst from his chest. Fear surged through him, and he scrambled to his feet. But at the exact moment, Kyle—now Aleks—intervened with astonishing speed.

A mighty flap of his majestic wings and he was down, his hand outstretched, fingers closing around Tyler, hoisting him clear of the ground. The force of their ascent whipped the air around them, a sure sign of the new power at Aleks' command. Below, the woman threw herself out onto the twisted wreckage of the car. She used the wreck as a springboard, allowing her to leap upward into the air toward Aleks and Tyler. Determined to bring them down, her knife was out and ready to strike its target.

"Look out!" Tyler cried in warning as he watched the woman ascend with lethal grace. In a fluid motion, Aleks countered, his sword meeting hers in a clash that halted her advance. The collision of their blades sent back a shockwave, stopping her momentum.

In another quick move, Aleks twisted in midair, his wings artfully using the currents before finally sending them soaring into the safety of the night sky. Down below, the woman remained alone among the car debris—now upside down—with her silhouette reducing as Aleks and Tyler soared in the darkness; the short-term danger had been evaded, but the night was still uncertain.

CHAPTER FIFTEEN
THE DESTINED

The air was thinner and colder at such a high altitude. Making breathing much more of a chore for Tyler, one he wasn't keen on performing, especially given recent events. His body ached from the accident and adrenaline-induced panic right down to the bone; his head was fuzzy, surely because of the lack of oxygen in the night air. He tried desperately to regain his bearings and gain control of his mind and body, but they evaded him. The sound of whipping cold wind was the only discerning sensation he could grasp.

He wanted to look up to Kyle—or Aleks, whichever being held onto him now—and tell them they were squeezing his already sore ribs too tight, that every fiber in his being wanted to be put back on the ground—but he didn't have the fortitude. He could only manage to drift off into the frustration of his thoughts for now, allowing the cold winds to continue stinging his face.

*

Emerging from the depth of darkness, Tyler felt the cool embrace of water—its touch and invasion—filling every crevice of his being with the chilling dread that he was drowning. Panic surged; his eyes snapped open, arms flailing out in a desperate fight for life. A glimmer of moonlight above him danced on the water's surface, drawing him toward it. His survival instincts kick in and thrust him towards the light until he reaches the surface, inhaling the cold night air in gasps of breaths like it was manna from the heavens, a realization creeping over his mind as he looked about—he was in the Scotler Manor pool. Tyler swam to the edge of the pool, his eyes still scanning around him, trying to find Kyle, who lay lifeless next to the pool.

The remains of his shredded clothes still clinging to his form, where his wings once were. The sight was a shock of disbelief. *Kyle isn't dead.* As still as Kyle was, Tyler clung to the thought with what remained of his might. His mind kept pulling up images of the night—of Kyle's ascension, his power. *He can't be dead.*

James's urgent voice cut through Tyler's concentration on Kyle. "Tyler!" From behind the glass of the manor, inside the kitchen, his voice came. James was a blur of motion, poolside faster than Tyler's eyes could follow. Kodi was right there with him, right by Kyle's side. It seemed as if, in one motion, Kyle's body was in the arms of Kodi. Tyler couldn't take his eyes off the body as James pulled him from the pool. "Tyler, what's going on?" James's voice punctured through Tyler's daze of shock.

"Someone in the road…" The words fell out of Tyler's mouth. Inside the manor, Kodi had already laid Kyle's body over the stone table and was asking one of the workers in the kitchen to bring him towels. "He can't be dead, right?" Tyler asks, shivering in his wet clothes.

"Tyler, tell me what happened," James said, his hand on Tyler's shoulders.

"After we left, we were headed up the canyon. The weather was bad." Tyler began. He could not stand looking away from Kyle, hoping for the slightest flutter of his eyes, "Something felt off. A woman was standing in the middle of the road with a knife. She slashed one of the rear tires, and Kyle lost control of the car…" Tyler stopped as the kitchen staff came back inside. Kodi passed Tyler a towel and gently put one under Kyle's head. Diana and Caleb entered behind the staff with more towels. Just as Kyle started to stir, a tiny movement of consciousness. Tyler huffed, his breath audible. He breathed out, realizing the breath had been trapped inside. He wasn't sure there was any more breath in him. *He's alive.*

Kyle clung to the amulet around his neck and murmured, "Aleks." Before falling back into unconsciousness.

Diana begins to assess Kyle as he drifts off.

"Kodi, Caleb, see if you can find some dry clothes for them both," Diana said.

Meanwhile, James pulled out his phone and put it to his ear. "Rebecca, they are here. Come to the manor." His words reverberate through Tyler's ears, injecting a fresh dose of reality into the surreal events of the night. Once the call ended, James appeared before Tyler again, "Try and remember exactly what happened. Where is the wrecked car?" Tyler was silent as he tried to piece the shards of his memory back together.

"James, Caleb, and I will find the wreckage," Diana interjected. James nodded and agreed with Diana's plan as Caleb and Kodi returned with clothes.

"Kodi, help Kyle to one of the guest rooms." Kodi nods and swiftly cradles Kyle's body. As Diana and Caleb depart to find the wreckage, Tyler follows closely behind Kodi and James to a guest room down the hall. The room was similarly decorated to the space Tyler was used to upstairs. Tyler was numb, only feeling the tingling sensation in his cold limbs.

He left Kyle's room with a change of dry clothes, eager to free his body from the damp entrapment. A cascade of emotions cloaked his mind—the weight of the night pressing down on him. The ride to the canyon, the wrecked car, and the woman on the road all orbited his mind. If what James said was true and they had truly arrived, then he was going to put up a damned good fight.

When Tyler went back into Kyle's room, James stood in silence. Tyler approached him, and both looked down at Kyle's still body. "We just wanted to find some normalcy," Tyler said. James faced him, his expression worrisome.

"Kyle will recover; the amulet he wears protects him." James said, "As he becomes more acquainted with his alternate self, the transition will get easier." His eyes turned from the amulet to James as the image of that being Tyler had seen come forth from Kyle's body returned to him so vividly. "Could I maybe use it for protection and save everyone else?" he asked, his voice carrying a curiosity to explore in atonement for Kyle's injury.

James shook his head. "You already possess a powerful artifact," he replied, pointing to the ring encircling Tyler's finger. "It doesn't function like the jewel bestowed to the Alexos. But, the royals, like yourself, received different gifts."

"How do I use it? What can I do to help?" He asked, the

weight of his responsibility in his voice. James just smiled, meeting Tyler's eyes.

"You are of royal blood, Tyler. Protection for you is a part of our very existence. The power that the royal family has at their fingertips is without limit. Soon, you will learn to wield it just as those before you did." James fell silent momentarily as if he were reaching a new realization. "What did this woman in the road look like?" He asked.

Tyler hesitated, remembering the vision. "Black hair, dressed in black with a dark laugh," he replied. "Do you have any idea who she is?"

James's face clouded, eyes shutting with a nod.

"I do, unfortunately," he replied, his voice low. "She is Raven Blaq—a guard to the Cerif." His words were black pillars in the room, and as he and Tyler stood in silence, the presence of the Cerif had arrived.

CHAPTER SIXTEEN

THE MIDNIGHT RAIN

In the dimly lit room, Tyler sat at Kyle's bedside reading more of the journal: *The smell of blood, the cover of night—True Vampire swallows the intoxicating delight…*As Tyler read the passage, a soft groan broke the silence. Kyle's eyelids fluttered open, his voice weak, "Are you okay?" He asked as Tyler met his gaze. Given Kyle's current state and personality, it was a likely role reversal.

"Shouldn't I be the one asking you that?" Tyler answered, his voice laced with relief and worry at the same time. He had half a mind to ask Kyle about whoever had come from the jade amulet nestled in gold around his neck and took over his body, but the sound of Kyle's voice deterred the thought.

"I'm sure you want to know about Aleks. Every chosen Alexos contains an alternate self, a protector of the Connected Key." It was almost as unbelievable as James had put it.

"This journal just keeps spewing riddles. I want to know about the other artifacts. Maybe in the study," the thought materialized faster than Tyler could speak as he stood from the chair beside Kyle's bed, heading for the door. "I'm glad you're awake, Ky. I have to recheck the study. I'll be right back." he added, heading out of the room.

Now that Tyler knew he was safe, or at least on the mend, he could turn his focus back to finding more answers. He walked the long hall to the kitchen, where the workers were fast at work preparing a meal: fresh vegetables, cuts of meat, seasonings, and—something else—large amounts of the red liquid poured into smaller containers from a bucket. Tyler recognized the look of it: metallic, dark red, with a pungent smell. It must have been in its raw form before being aerated, as Phoenix described in the writings.

What was its origin? What living thing was robbed of

its essence to sustain another? The sight was gut-wrenching. Tyler didn't dare ask, not now. There was enough revelation to reconcile with.

The manor was quiet as Tyler roamed up to the study. Once engulfed in the sea of books, he scanned the titles with text he could understand. One caught his eye: a book with a singular imprint that looked like the wax seal stamped on the envelope that enclosed the ring he now wore—a prominent letter "V" intricately entwined within its design. As Tyler opened it and turned its pages, he arrived at a sketch of a family dressed in royal clothing, none of whom Tyler recognized, but a young woman with dark hair stood out. The features of her face were reminiscent of the face he saw last night, a ghost from the past. The entrance of James and Kodi into the study broke Tyler's concentration, and the atmosphere changed. Tyler swiveled around to face them, his finger on the woman in the sketched image. "Who is this woman?" he asked.

James approached him, taking the book into his hands. "She was once a royal family member, like yourself." He replied. Tyler's brow furrowed, waiting for further explanation.

Kodi approached beside them, looking at the sketch. "Now she's trying to kill us." He said sharply, confirming Tyler's suspicions. It was indeed the woman from the road.

"But why? Who is she?" Tyler pleaded again. James returned the book to Tyler, crossing the room and sitting behind the large wooden desk. Tyler sat at the desk but still waited for his question to be answered.

"Raven Asoron, as she was known then—your father's cousin." James's voice was stone-cold as his eyes bored into Tyler's, "her blood was tainted, severing her connection to the royal Vasilikós bloodline." Kodi approached the shelves on the opposite side of the room, pulling another book from high up on its shelves. It was larger and thicker than most others in the library. He opened it on the desk, flipping its pages confidently as though he were familiar with its contents.

Once he was done, he spun the book on the desk to Tyler. "She and another gifted blood were recruited to join the Cerif," James added. Another sketch of a man and a woman was on the book's page. Tyler recognized this woman—it was Diana and a familial man beside her. "My uncle, Solomon De-

Garr," Kyle said as if responding to Tyler's curious thoughts.

"But why them? I don't understand," Tyler asked, his gaze lifting from the open page. His fears thickened the air, deepening the mystery into family, trust, loyalty, and power. Again, Tyler wrestled with the chilling realization: his own family had defected to the enemy's side to become part of the Cerif Guard. James leaned forward, his eyes reflecting the gravity of his forthcoming words.

"Every member of the Cerif Guard had been chosen with deliberate purpose," he began. "Each one had a tie to the royal bloodline—Solomon, for example, a Shafeir—his blood runs strong with the mixture of royal and vampire. Raven bore the royal bloodline, and her lover, Brody, is tied to the whispers of the dark." Tyler heard the thud of his heartbeat in his ears as James' words sank in. The thought of what it would mean for the safety of those he loved should he continue the path to his supposed destiny, making them potential targets in the evil chess game he found himself part of.

"My aunt and uncle. They are in danger."

James shook his head, "I've asked them to stay where

they are. We are being watched."

Watched? Tyler stirred with curiosity and concern. "James, what are the Cerif Guard capable of exactly?" Tyler asked, "Her swords, are they ancient artifacts, too?"

James shook his head, a faint, grim smile pulling at the corner of his lips. "No, her swords grant her no additional strength. It is the blood that courses through her that gives her vampiric speed, strength, and the distinct mark of a True Vampire—red eyes." As Tyler's eyes shifted from James, some movement caught his eye in the large window beyond the desk.

To his surprise, a pair of sinister, crimson-red eyes stared at him, belonging to the figure of a woman somehow suspended midair. The room's peace was shattered as the woman's hand smashed through the window, glass cascading like a crystal waterfall. "Take Tyler to the safe room, now!" James shouted as he stood to face the menace closing in on them. "She can't enter. Go, now!" Kodi nodded and guided Tyler through the halls of the manor.

They were soon in the dining room, where Kodi approached a portrait hanging on the wall. He pulled it aside, revealing a hidden metal door. He started punching a code into a tiny keypad before there was clicking from locks echoing throughout the room. Then, the door slowly swung open, revealing an illuminated staircase to an underground bunker. Kodi guided Tyler down them and into the cool space.

"You'll be safe down here for now," Kodi said as more lights flicked on, reacting to their presence. The bunker was a stark contrast to the elegance of Scotler Manor; its walls were lined with metal and cement. From the staircase, it opened up to a large furnished area, with one wall shelved with more books. There were ancient trunks and mounted screens on the other wall. Opposite them was a line of closed doors. "Hold on here, I'll get Kyle," Kodi said, charging up the stairs. It was only a second before he returned with Kyle, still limping from his body's transformation.

"What's happening?" Kyle gasped, his voice tinged with pain and confusion.

"That woman from the road…she's here," Tyler answered. Kodi stood at the threshold of the staircase, a look of worry crossing his face. "What is it, Kodi?" Tyler asked.

"I can feel Caleb. He and my mom must be close," he replied. Before Tyler's lips could move to respond, Kodi was off and running up the stairs, the locks on the heavy metal door clicking into place behind him as he went, sealing them within. Tyler, in this underground sanctuary, was left to wonder about the turmoil unfolding above, his mind a whirlwind of worry for James, Kodi, Caleb, and Diana.

They moved toward the array of monitors on the wall. No word was said, but the air between the two was tense. Determined to know what was happening above, Tyler went to the control panel on the desk and brought the screens to life. It showed the angles of Scotler Manor's exterior. Outside was portrayed in each feed. Tyler's fingers danced across the keys, and the scene snapped into sharpness—he'd spent a whole semester of his first year in high school working in the backstage theatre club.

The audio feed crackled then cleared, and they could now hear the confrontation blaring from the monitor's through hidden speakers. James stood square-set and firm in the manor's courtyard below the study on one of the screens, voice booming across the bunker, "Raven, this isn't the path you were meant to walk."

Raven scoffed back.

"There are no more choices, James. My loyalty is with the Cerif, and my orders are clear. I am to take the boy to them. My hate for you and those you call royal remains intact." Tyler couldn't look away from the screen as Raven and James suddenly launched into a fury of rapid blows at one another—the dance of power and desperation. Tyler noticed Raven's weapons remained stowed, which was either an act of strategy or something more. Kodi stood close by, another line of defense.

Diana and Caleb joined the fight, bursting onscreen from the tree line. Diana moved with the vengeance of any mother and wife as James threw Raven off him again. They were standing beside James in a flash, Diana, Caleb, and Kodi, as Diana shouted above the noise, "Another vampire is close!" Her eyes closed for only a moment, "On your left!"

The video feed to the bunker cut out right then.

"What happened?" Kyle yelled in anticipation. Tyler scrambled, his fingers flying over the keyboard again to get the feedback back. Moments later, the picture returned. It showed James mid-leap as he intercepted a new figure from the tree line. But the figure dodged the attack, moving at twice the speed of the others, appearing beside Raven in seconds.

"You show weakness, James," a smooth cold voice declared. Now, in clear view, the figure was all too recognizable to Tyler—the man from the sketch in the book. Solomon DeGarr. James spun to face the members of the Cerif Guard standing before his family and out of reach.

Raven launched another attack, her agility, and malice on full display. "You can't fend us both off forever!" she sneered as she flew into a high kick, her body whirling with the movement. Solomon joined, targeting James, who ran full speed to defend his family. But as they collided, James, like an acrobat, eluded the attack and leaped backward with unnatural skill and sheer will. Tyler watched in awe from the safety of the bunker, surging with frustration.

"We need to do something, Ky," he exclaimed.

Kyle put a comforting hand on Tyler's shoulder. "I can't summon Aleks right now. My body took a beating the first time, but don't worry. They're experienced. Let them do their duty." The feeling of it all dropped off as the battle intensified by the second. Kodi and Caleb confronted Solomon, keeping up with his speed while Raven, her red eyes burning like hot coals, pulled her dagger from her side. With the cackle of her chilling laugh again, she threw the black blade that sought Diana's life. James was quick to respond, but fate was swifter.

"Diana!" he called out, as the dagger struck Diana before he could reach her. The impact sent shockwaves through the bunker, and Tyler and Kyle could only watch in horror. Raven's evil roar continued to pour out from the bunker speakers, and even Solomon showed a flicker of conflict upon seeing his sister's fall.

"Raven, it's time to retreat," he commanded as the Scotler twins retreated from his confrontation to the aid of their mother. "The boy is beyond our reach here. We wait for another opportunity. Let's go." Still caught up in her triumph, Raven hesitated, her gaze lingering on the immediate pain she caused. Finally, following Solomon's command, she withdrew, leaving the manor and its guardians to reckon with the havoc of the Cerif Guard.

CHAPTER SEVENTEEN
THE DUSKY ROSE

Outside Scotler Manor, a storm raged, like the reflection of the destruction left in the wake of the True Vampire's appearance. It was as if the elements were reacting to the departure of Raven and Solomon, whipping them into a frenzy. The tension was palpable inside. Tyler, anxious beyond measure, paced the concrete floors of the bunker, each footstep reverberating off the sterile walls. He and Kyle waited desperately for the return of the family that protected them from the vampires.

Tyler's eyes frequently lifted to the bolted door at the top of the stairs, a barrier between him and the unknown fate of Diana, whose situation he couldn't begin to imagine. Still wounded, Kyle did what he could to settle the brewing storm inside the bunker—his voice level as he spoke to soothe Tyler. "What we saw on those screens…it might not be as bad as it looked," he said, fingers absentmindedly toying with the amulet around his neck.

His words did little to settle Tyler's spiraling thoughts.

"You're all risking your lives…for me," Tyler murmured, his voice layered with guilt. He couldn't shake the image of Diana being struck with the dagger Raven threw from his mind.

Kyle crossed the room to the bookshelves, his back to Tyler. "History says that the Shafeir and Alexos would sacrifice themselves when needed to protect the royals," he explained, his tone scholarly as he pulled a dusty book from the shelf.

"I refuse to be helpless. I want to fight alongside everyone else," Tyler declared, firmly determined to no longer stay on the sidelines. Kyle turned back to him and nodded in understanding before turning to the ancient book and flipping through it. "These symbols… I can't make anything of them,"

Kyle said. Tyler came closer to the bookshelf and took the book in hand. They were cryptic symbols that he recognized, the same ones he had seen in the journal, and like the journal, they began to transform before his eyes. A message deciphered: *…born of blood both royal and dead…Shafeir…*

"Wait, I can read this," Tyler began but was cut off by the echoing release of bolts from the door at the top of the stairs. Tyler handed the book to Kyle and sprinted for the staircase, where James was coming down with Diana's body. It was a gut-wrenching sight: Diana's bloodied clothes, the twins—Kodi and Caleb—marked by the violence that had come upon them. James had her up in his arms and took her through one of the closed doors in the bunker. Behind it was a small bedroom where he laid her down with such gravity that the room filled with a mournful silence.

Unable to speak, Tyler watched as James directed his sons to gather supplies for Diana's care. His heart sank when Tyler finally saw the black dagger still protruding from Diana's belly. He couldn't bring himself to ask what would become of Diana.

"What about the dagger?" Kyle asked in a hushed voice.

Tyler was glad Kyle had the strength to ask the hard truths. James stood up by the bedside, his voice weighted with hopelessness. "It cannot be removed…not yet. The dagger Raven threw was a product of dark magic, poisoned by her lover, Brody," he explained in a cocktail of grief and resolve. Tyler wanted so badly to apologize for the danger they were in.

"James, I am so—"

"There's nothing to be sorry for." Kodi's voice was sharp and brisk as he returned with all the essentials to care for Diana. "Our sworn duty is to protect the royal bloodline."

Kodi added.

"That is what matters. You are safe, and the Cerif cannot breach these walls for now." His eyes briefly met Kodi's. "And as for Diana…she will pull through if we can keep her stable," he trailed off. Then, realization struck Tyler.

"Blood," he murmured, the sound of realization and revulsion in his voice as he remembered the stores of the red fluid he'd seen the kitchen staff handling.

James replied with stern clarity, "Yes, blood. But be assured that we only consume the blood of animals when necessary. It gives us vitality and satiates our vampiric urges in a way that other sustenance cannot." Tyler was relieved that the blood was not cruelly sourced, but he felt a hint of shame in the back of his mind for assuming so. Caleb returned to the room with clean clothes for his mother, his voice wafting into the room with simmering frustration.

"I hope you didn't think that fight was our best. Solomon wouldn't have stood a chance if Kodi and I were at our full strength." He mused.

James was quick to quell such talk with a sharp tone. "Caleb, you know well enough when that time will come." His command for silence was clear. Soon after James exited the room holding his phone, Tyler couldn't catch his hushed and urgent conversation. Only James's last words drifted back, "Cassandra, we need you. They came, it's time."

*

As it got late and the quiet of the night crept in, Tyler was in a room next to Diana's with only a small lamp for light.

The book Kyle discovered and the journal that was given to him by James at his side. James insisted everyone stay in the bunker and not be alone for the night. Kyle protested the idea, wanting to check on his mother at home, but James contacted Patricia, Rebecca, and Rion himself—they agreed with James. Tyler read from the book Kyle found once more, continuing where he left off…*there were five, born to one. Royal by blood and equal to none. A mother stricken with fear for the cause of sum. Children now in darkness plagued by the sun. Cursed by the mother, two live forever as one. The gift of blood, their salvation undone…until years overcome…royalty threatened a kingdom exposed in requiem. Derived from the mother's blood, both royal and dead, Shafeir by name—new beings were bred. Sentinels of the Vasilikós, a bond hinged on the fruits of ties—in ceremony, it is given—in blood, it lies…*

The words cast a stillness in the room as if they demanded silence for the story to be told. Tyler's eyes were glued to the words spun on the pages until a startling thud at the door jolted him from focus, his eyes shooting up to the door. It opened to a familiar face, Kyle. His entry broke the silent trance as he spoke, "Figured it all out yet?" He asked, his gaze on the open book as he shut the door behind him. With a heavy sigh, Tyler looked down at the pages again, shaking his head.

"It's all here, Ky. The truth about the blood of the royals, a gifting ceremony…it's all part of some bond, the power exchange with the Shafeir. But what if…what if I am just a pawn in all this?" Tyler's tone was grave, his expression dark.

Kyle sat next to Tyler on the small bed. "I hear you, but from what I know of True Vampires, they're known for their lies and thirst for power. They want control."

Tyler nodded in agreement, his thoughts filled with doubt and suspicion. "But what if the real enemy are claiming to protect us now? What if the actual danger is closer than we think?"

Kyle's expression became questionable, pondering Tyler's words. "No matter what, we stick together, right? Side by side, no matter what happens. I don't know if you can trust anything written in that book, but there had to be a reason it was there, right? So we'll figure it out." The strength of their friendship was comforting in the presence of so much uncertainty. Tyler was grateful to have his friend back. He was happy that their pact remained and would not have to bear his pain alone as he moved forward through the shadowed corridors ahead. But doubt and the potential for deception remained. Were they indeed those who said they were, the Shafeir and Alexos?

CHAPTER EIGHTEEN

THE OVERTURE

Tyler jolted upright, snapping awake, the book sliding off his chest in the process. He had been sitting up against the small bed in the bunker. The small lamp still lit the room dimly, and the murmur of voices poured in from beneath the bedroom door—familiar tones. As Tyler flipped the book away and out of his way to get out of bed, he opened the door to familiar faces that matched the sound of the voices. Sitting in the space of the bunker was his aunt Rebecca, wearing a peculiar scarf with a floral print around her neck. His uncle Rion was seated next to her. They sat opposite Kyle and James on furniture in the middle of the room.

"Good morning, Tyler," Rebecca said, her voice a soothing balm as Tyler approached. She and Rion stood, embracing Tyler before sitting again.

"You're here," Tyler said with a curious smile.

"We had to come to see you all were okay," Rion replied.

"Most of this morning, I was with Diana," Rebecca said, looking to the ajar door of Diana's recovery room, her voice lingering with concern, "and, of course, when we heard Cassandra was coming." Tyler's mind raced back to the cryptic phone call James made, connecting the dots between the sudden arrival of his guardians and the name James uttered that night, Cassandra.

"Who's Cassandra?"

What followed each of Tyler's questions was becoming a consistent pattern: an exchange of glances and a dead silence. Until, at last, Rion waves him over, inviting him to sit on his left and join the group. "Cassandra's my sister. That is who I called," James said. Tyler's head flicked in his direction.

"She is also Rennon's guardian," Rebecca added suddenly as if ripping off a band aide—which she successfully did—uncovering a torrent of emotions cascading through Tyler's mind. The first wave was of excitement for reuniting with the brother he never knew he had. Uncertainty of what the reunion would bring, and then numbness, the news too overwhelming for Tyler to fathom. Tyler's mind drifted to Diana, and his eyes fell onto the open door of her bedroom, an anchor to their harsh reality: he was greeted with the visual of IVs pumping life-sustaining blood directly into her veins.

"How will this reunion help Diana?" He asked.

"When they arrive, we can discuss the details."

James replied.

Tyler was beginning to feel like the bunker's walls were caving in on him. Suddenly, the vast space was overcrowded, and he had to leave. Mumbling an answer to James and the others, he pushed himself off the couch and went up the steps. Before long, he was out of the cage and back up in the world that the metal door had opened him to, bathed in the morning air with the scent of a prepared breakfast, which offered a semblance of normalcy back into his life that he believed would never return.

In the kitchen, the chef worked diligently preparing the breakfast spread. On the dining table, a setting much like the first dinner Tyler experienced at the manor. Only this time with glasses of the red liquid for those partook in the essence. The sunlight poured in beyond the table, and the heat of the rays pushed Tyler to the glass window, the gateway to the courtyard and pool, alive with the memories of that which he had seen on the screens in the bunker--now peaceful and orderly in the quiet of morning light. Tyler was at a crossroads, seized between worlds of calmness and chaos, as he again entered into yet another new chapter of life.

*

In the ambiance of the breakfast table, the sound of clinking cutlery and the soft murmur of conversation layered in the background. Tyler sat with his thoughts a whirlpool of anticipation and jitters about the imminent reunion with his twin brother, Rennon. Tyler's gaze met Rebecca's across the table, the moment inspiring a question that poured from his lips. "Does Rennon know about…our world?" Tyler asked, his voice barely a whisper amid the morning buzz. Rebecca's gaze swept the room, the repetitive dance of glances and silence before she nodded in response.

"He does." She replied with a confirmation that settled like a weight on Tyler's chest, the imbalance of shared knowledge between them gnawing at him. *Why him and not me?* He pondered silently, the thought souring his appetite as he pushed away from the table. Tyler knew this wasn't the moment to voice his concerns—the focus was saving Diana. So, he turned and left without a word, the soft scrape of the chair across the hard floor marking his exit. Kyle followed Tyler's footsteps into the sanctuary of the next room and sat on the long white couch with him.

"I know what you're thinking, Ty, but you should see what I found in the study," Kyle said, standing before retreating to the staircase. Tyler followed his steps, intrigued. In the study, surrounded by the towering shelves of books, Kyle pulled book after book into his arms. "I was up most of the night after you told me your theory," he said, bringing the tomes to Tyler.

"What have you dug up, Professor Huntington?" Tyler asked, a nickname of Kyle's insatiable search for knowledge. Kyle smirked, ignoring the name, and opened the books, flipping their pages and spinning them around for Tyler to see. "What am I looking at?"

"More of the same—other than this, my research was interrupted when I stumbled upon these symbols like the ones in the other book we found in the bunker." Tyler leaned over the open pages, once again triggering the changing of the foreign symbols before his eyes…*upon the twilight of the moon, under eye of the cosmos itself—the mother. Gemini born, they were, twice gifted twofold of unparalleled might. A new era of enlightenment or despair, too immense for the young souls to bear…*

…for in their eyes a torment burns, I fear the gifted blood cannot be contained. Dear Mother—our cosmos be, bless them reprieve for we, your royal children, cannot…

…our pleas go unheard by Mother. The power promised has damned us all, twice blessed and twice cursed—a fusion blurred into singularity. Pain…torment…betrayal…love, cloaked by

shadow. A descent into madness, they are, my kin…

The words sent chills into the air as he spoke them out loud—a destiny connected to the presence of the Gemini twins, igniting the fear of a doomed fate. "Do you think this is why you and Rennon have been separated?" Kyle asked. The silence in the room was deafening as Tyler thought through what the text meant for him and his long-lost twin. "Ty, are you going to let the others know?" Kyle asked. Tyler shook his head.

"I don't think I will," Tyler began to flip the book's pages. "Obviously, whoever wrote in these books intended for it only to be read by someone in the royal bloodline." He glanced from the book, locking eyes with Kyle. "You have to promise not to say anything, Ky," he said firmly. Kyle drew a long breath and measured his words. Tyler slammed the book shut on the table, looking further into Kyle's eyes.

"Of course, I won't."

CHAPTER NINETEEN

THE CONNECTED

Time drifted, as elusive as the whispering of the past in the heavy air of the study—like a silent symphony. Tyler was swamped in a sea of words, leather-bound and worn. He did not take notice of Kyle's comings and goings, whose presence and accompanying whispers wisped past him like a constant clock ticking as he came and went from the study…*I pled with Drëi, but I fear the darkness has corrupted him—that vampire filth poisoning his mind, no doubt. Not the purpose of the Connected Key…my dear Drëi and Aïra…*

Tyler's reading came to a halt again as a gentle tap on his shoulder drew him from the page. Kyle handed him the journal he left in the bunker before disappearing from the study again. He ran his fingers over the worn cover of the journal before paging through it. They shared no further text on the blank pages. "I need to find the rest of the story," he said. As his mind wandered, the names from the page slipped from his lips. "Drėi and Aïra." The names spoken aloud caused the room to stir—the pages of the journal Tyler held in his hands shuffled under a wind he could not feel but see the effects of, stopping at another blank page.

Those who seek truth shall find it.

Beware the darkness, do not incite it.

The words materialized from strange symbols before fading, leaving the page blank again. "What are you?" Tyler inquired, addressing the ancient journal like a living confidant. The only reply was a cryptic greeting.

Hello, Tyler Asoron.

The ink bled through the page, only this time lingering as he read it. A greeting from a book, Tyler felt like he had been buried alive with these books for just too long, and it was time to come up for air. He snapped the journal shut, and then the others gathered for him along with it. He rose from the wooden desk and went to the study's door. One step after another, he crawled out of the burial, only to find Kyle's concerned eyes on the other side of the door.

"Where are you wandering off to?" Kyle asked.

"I just need to get out of here for a while. What time is it?" Tyler replied.

"Well, let's not wander off alone, especially right now," Kyle insisted, "everyone is in the bunker with Diana. I'll go with you." His voice was tinged with concern and under-standing of what danger might be lurking around.

"You're probably right, but are you sure you're up for it?" Tyler asked, mindful of what happened the last time Kyle accompanied him on one of his adventures.

Kyle nodded, reassured, "I'm nearly back to my old self—benefits of an Alexos."

*

The moment Tyler stepped out into the cool, humid air,

a freeing breath filled his lungs, almost as though he breathed in life itself, somehow leaving the secrets of the study to simmer in his absence. Walking alongside Kyle, their footsteps harmonized with an earthy crunch beneath them—eyes closed, Tyler heightened his other senses—an escape that was much needed. Kyle's voice was the only thing that now violated the peaceful silence as they continued along the dirt path, entering the forest surrounding the manor. "I guess because I was born into this supernatural world, it was only a matter of time before I had to face my destiny. I can't imagine ever being thrown into it like you have, Ty," he said solemnly.

His words pulled Tyler back into the turbulence that was his life again.

"Feels like everyone and everything in my life has been a lie," Tyler replied, his head low as he thumbed the ring on his finger, "And now I'm supposed to master being the Connected Key with my brother, defeat a vampire coven, and restore balance to some kingdom I've never known—all while just trying to live to see high school graduation with my best friend."

"I know what you mean there," Kyle said, kicking a small stone on the dirt path. Tyler was sure Kyle did know what he meant, being his sworn Alexos protector. He empathized with him, yet a lingering thought had been steering Tyler towards a doubtful theory.

"Ky, was our meeting and friendship all a lie, too?"

He and Kyle walked in silence, with their heads low. Tyler glanced to his friend, seeing the flash of pain wash over his face before the silence was finally broken. "No. I wish I could have told you everything about me and my family sooner, but I couldn't. Part of me was still accepting it all myself." Their synchronized steps trailed to a stop. Tyler could hear the sincerity in Kyle's voice. He believed Kyle truly would have told him if he could, but the layers of doubt and betrayal still ached within, the cuts too deep.

"I understand."

"We should probably get back," Kyle said, checking their surroundings. Tyler's reality continued flooding back, intensifying the looming dread of confronting his altered new life.

*

The open and liberating outdoors to the manor's weight solidifies Tyler's reality. Inside, James, the Scotler twins, and Rion were in the family room. James stood against the door frame in the kitchen, a glass of the red liquid in hand—still an unsettling sight for Tyler, a reminder of the unnerving changes he had yet to get used to. Rion and the Scotler twins sat on the long white sofas, their gaze focused on Tyler and Kyle as they entered. "Everything okay?" Rion asked. Tyler and Kyle exchanged a glance nodding.

"Ky and I needed some air."

James drew a sip of the red liquid from the glass. Tyler watched as he savored it before swallowing. He imagined what it must taste like, the aerated liquid of an animal. "Rebecca and I were worried," Rion added.

"Where is she?" Tyler asked.

"In the bunker with Diana," James licked the red residue from his lips. Tyler nodded, crossing the room to the kitchen doorway. The sound of a ringtone stopped him, and James fumbled in his pocket as the sound continued echoing. He finally pulled the buzzing phone from his pocket and answered it. It didn't take long for Tyler to realize who the caller was.

It was Cassandra, and she was in tears.

"Slow down," James said, sitting the glass on the countertop. I can't understand you." Cassandra's breath was so loud Tyler could hear it from the receiver. He moved closer to James, curious what she had to say. James pulled the phone from his ear and put it on speakerphone. "What happened, Cassandra?" he asked calmly.

"Listen, when I told Ren about Tyler and the recent attack from the Cerif, he ran off."

James met Tyler's eyes as Cassandra spoke before replying calmly. "He will come back. Go after him if he doesn't. It's dangerous for them both right now." Tyler didn't notice when the phone call ended. The moment he heard Cassandra's words, his world spun. Her words blurred into muffled audio as Tyler went spiraling. The rug once again ripped out from under him, a never-ending climb he would now face alone.

"What happened?" Kyle's voice broke into the room.

James explained the call from Cassandra, "It seems Rennon is not too thrilled about joining us here." Tyler balled his fists, hearing the words again, so tight that his fingers hurt. But any pain he felt paled in comparison to what was inside, knowing that his brother, of all living beings, knows of his existence and need of him and chooses not to help. It hurt. Throbbed in his chest, so much so that his eyes were beginning to burn.

Finally, Tyler stormed back into the room, the pain becoming fuel as he fought through the emotions.

"It's fine—he doesn't owe me or any of us anything," Tyler proclaimed, the time for protection from his reality suddenly ending. Tyler needed to learn and train independently to protect himself and prepare for whatever was coming next. The room was silent as Tyler's words absorbed into the air. But Tyler didn't have time to think, to ponder the decisions and thoughts of others. He headed for the staircase set on returning to his studies.

Behind him, James and Rion's voices rose in a mix of concern and confusion, but their words dissolved into the air before reaching his ears as he entered the study. He was surprised Kodi, Caleb, and Kyle so closely trailed his steps.

"What are you going to do, Ty?" Kyle asked.

With trembling hands, Tyler flipped open the journal again. Words, like desperate pleas, spill from his lips, "Give me some straight answers! What am I supposed to do?" Every command he shouted fell flat on the mute pages. His frustration becomes a living thing, filling the room with something solid, something that could almost be touched. The others watched in rapt silence.

Suddenly, from nowhere, an ethereal light began to pour from the journal's spine. Instantly, the ring on Tyler's finger blazed with light and vibrations, reacting to the journal's light. The light shimmered, and reality warped as a spectral presence coalesced, woven through every nook and cranny of the study. "What's happening?" Tyler shouted, overwhelmed by an indescribable force. Tyler felt his senses reel, his grip on reality loosening, the study transforming into a vortex of swirling light, the figures of his friends fading, converging in a symphony of mystic energy as Tyler's consciousness teeters on the brink before plunging into an abyss of open darkness.

CHAPTER TWENTY

THE PARADOX

The sound of waves crashing in the distance brought Tyler's senses into sharp focus, unveiling an unfamiliar reality: an uneven, wet surface below him—and a voice cutting through the ambient noise of the sea.

"Rennon? Rennon, can you hear me?"

The voice called out, urgent and concerned. It wandered closer and further away as if searching for him. Tyler was trapped in darkness still, an unyielding internal battle, thoughts running in his mind: *Who is that? Why am I not moving? Why can't I speak?* He was almost shouting, and this time, his inaudible voice echoed, still running away into the vast emptiness of his mind with no response. Finally, light seeped through opening eyelids, turning the dark world into one of blurred colors and shapes.

Tyler was on a shoreline. A woman's figure appeared, eclipsing the light above him. Her features slowly came into focus—short blonde hair, big expressive hazel eyes, and a look on her face that was pure fear and worry. "Rennon, what in God's name were you thinking, running off like that?" she said, her voice laced with relief. "Are you hurt?" Tyler suddenly recognized the tone of voice as Cassandra Scotler's from the phone call with James. His sister and guardian of—Tyler tried desperately again to speak, to correct the woman calling him by his brother's name.

He finally finds the will to say a few words: "I am not Rennon," he manages, the sound of his voice alien to his ears.

Cassandra jerked back a bit, her face changing to one of confusion. "Not Rennon?" she repeated her tone a mixture of curiosity and disbelief. "Tyler?"

Tyler could manage a slight nod. It was more a gesture of acknowledgment and a plea to have her believe. Cassandra's eyes opened wide as revelation and understanding struck her. She helped him up from the cold, damp shore, quick in motion, assisting Tyler to a parked car nearby. "This is incredible. You are already more powerful than I thought…projecting your consciousness into Rennon's body? It is something of the old tales," she added, sitting Tyler in the backseat of the car.

As they settled in the car, Tyler caught a glimpse of himself in the rearview mirror, confronted by the shocking reflection of a face not his own. Cassandra meets his gaze in the mirror with intrigue. "The Gemini connection, the twin bond…if you've connected with the journal and the artifact as Rennon has connected with his artifact, then perhaps…perhaps this is just the beginning," she said thoughtfully, starting the car and pulling away from the rocky beach, the sound of the waves dwindling into silence.

At the fall of the dimming light of the day, Tyler's fight for a voice continued, more tangible, as he rode in the confines of the car. "His…ring?" he managed, the sound barely a whisper lost in the hum of the car's engine.

Cassandra's gaze was fixed down the curving road before

them, her lips moving but her eyes not shifting from ahead. Her voice was calm but tinged with just an edge of something urgent. "Just try to relax for now. We need to get you somewhere safe," she said, the engine's roar revving a clear sign of her pressing the pedal. Tyler could feel the car gain speed, putting distance between them and whatever lurked in the night.

The ride was an attack on Tyler's senses, the car's movements amplifying his disorientation: this body he occupied was at the mercy of the car's every maneuver. Thrown off balance by a simple change in direction until defeated by inertia, slumped against the seat, a puppet severed from its strings. Night firmly settled in the sky, and Tyler found himself in darkness again, only seeing the occasional passing lights when, abruptly, the flare of multicolored lights gave the inside of the car a new glow. Under her breath, Cassandra cursed, a low hum of frustration as she eased the vehicle to a stop. "Not now," she snapped quietly, gripping the wheel with white-knuckled tension as she nervously adjusted the rearview mirror, meeting Tyler's concerned gaze in the backseat for a moment.

Looking in the rearview mirror, Tyler noticed Cassandra groaning as if in pain with the distinct noise of cracking bones or something. Tyler saw her slowly change, facial features twisted, a visible fight against the change she was going through. From blonde to brunette, hair extending, her eyes changed to a bright gold—the same haunting sight Tyler was all too familiar with and now knew it was the activation of a Shafeir's power. In horror and fascination, Tyler watched a chameleon adapt to a challenge.

The echo of heavy boots hit the road, coming closer to the car. A silhouetted, uniformed person crosses Tyler's sight through the back window. The flashlight beams a sign of the curious investigating party. The next sound was one of an electronic motor lowering Cassandra's car window. "Councilwoman—Ms. Jeffreys," a mellow voice said, a mix of respect and surprise. "We had a report of a vehicle matching this description driving erratically on these roads."

Tyler looked at the unfamiliar woman he knew as Cassandra as she brushed a lock of her long, dark hair over her shoulder. "Oh, I'm certain that wasn't me, I assure you, officer.

But I appreciate your vigilance," her tone was smooth, her voice altered to match the new appearance. She replied with such practiced ease, the embodiment of innocence.

The officer's flashlight sweeps over the car, pausing on Tyler's still form. "And him? Is he alright?" the curiosity in the officer's voice carried undertones of concern.

"He's just ill, a friend of my son's. I'm making sure he gets home safe," Cassandra fabricates effortlessly, her lie steeped in the veneer of concern matching the officers.

There was a silence before Tyler heard the click of the flashlight. "Take care of him," he says, a parting gesture of goodwill to him and the masked liar in the driver's seat. Footsteps trailed past Tyler again before the slam of a car door. Soon after, the roar of another engine ignites and passes by the humming parked car.

Once the two of them were alone, Cassandra's mask seemed to dissolve away, leaving her in her skin as she let out more groans of pain. "This gift," she began, her voice strained, "granted to me by my artifact." She motioned to a bracelet around her right wrist, the design ancient and intricate. "Is not without its toll on a weakened Shafeir." Tyler locked onto the object.

"Why?" he breathed, his voice only a whisper.

Her eyes met his in the mirror—with regret and resolve. "Survival," she said simply, the word heavy with an unspoken meaning. The car resumed its journey, the silence filled with the weight of Tyler's curiosities and questioning why the artifacts were given with such varying abilities and if his own would eventually reveal more to him. Soon, his thoughts slipped into a restful sleep, and a voice called out. "Casi."

"Rennon!" Cassandra exclaims, momentary focus drawn from the road. The car swerves—a dance with danger—before she regains control, her breaths coming in sharp gasps.

Tyler remains with that tug at the back of his mind, urging him toward an unseen place as the voice persists, "Get me to my brother." His presence in the body, not his own, fades away, relinquishing control to Rennon. Tyler's final question floats in his mind: would this mean a return to his body? Before he slips again into the engulfing dark, discovery is on the horizon.

CHAPTER TWENTY-ONE
THE MOLLIFICATION

Tyler's eyes slowly fluttered open to the familiar sight of the glow of the early morning sun shining through the windows of the guest bedroom at Scotler Manor. A sharp pain ran through him, reminding him he was still alive. Tyler looked over at the medical equipment sitting next to his bed. The tubes that came out of his body were white with clear liquid running from them into a bag, unlike Diana's red ones. Tyler groaned, his voice a mere whisper while trying to string together the pieces of his journey while observing the room.

He sees Kyle in a makeshift bed, stirring at the sound of his voice. His eyes blinked away the remnants of a restless sleep. "Hey," he whispers, "how do you feel?" With titanic effort, Tyler moves in the bed to prop himself up, his whole body protesting every twitch.

"Like I've been trampled by a herd of elephants," he jokes weakly, offering Kyle a faint smile. Kyle's face softens with relief, but his eyes betray his worry.

"You gave us quite the scare in the study with the whole glowing book and ring thing. When that light exploded, and you were floating there. It was like something out of a horror film." Tyler's brow furrowed as he absorbed Kyle's words, the memories returning in blurry flashes.

"No scientific explanation for that, eh? I…I was in Rennon's body, I'm pretty sure. I saw and heard everything he did." Kyle's eyes widen in disbelief.

"In Rennon's body? How? Are you sure it wasn't just a dream?" Before Tyler could respond, James and Caleb entered the room, their expressions concerned and curious. James breaks the growing tension with his commanding tone.

"You've been out for almost two days. We were starting to get worried."

"Two days?" Tyler repeats with disbelief. "So, I didn't come right back…" James nods solemnly, his gaze locking with Tyler's.

"What you experienced…it was a mind projection. A connection only twins have, and even then, it's rare. Especial-ly at such distance." Caleb leaned against the doorframe, his expression growing ever more curious.

"Kodi and I can feel each other, but nothing like what you just went through. Dad, how is this possible? Kodi and I can't do this."

"It's his royal blood," James explained. "The power that runs through their veins is ancient, potent—an exception to the rules. Shafeir only have a fraction of that strength. Tyler's link, the ancient power. It has always been dormant, never reached out to Rennon, until now, that is." Tyler's head has a pattern of interlocking clicks as he pieces it together.

"But why were we separated? Why was I not supposed to know about this?"

"To protect you. To protect the bloodline. After the king-dom fell, preserving the royal lineage became most important.

Your blood, the Connected Key, it's not just about power…
it's about balance." James said sternly. Tyler's eyes drift to the
window, heavy yet again with the weight of his heritage and
the gravity of his destiny. The room falls silent. Each person is
lost in their thoughts until Tyler breaks the silence again with
a question.

"Are Rebecca and Rion still here?"

"They are not," James replied, "they went to welcome
Cassandra and Rennon and should return soon." A reminder of the coming reunions awakened the emotions trapped
in Tyler's body. His thoughts turned to the confrontation, to
the unresolved tensions between him and Rennon, and to the
looming threats about them. Rennon's initial decision not to
join him still hadn't settled well.

*

As the night descended and the light became exclusively
that of the single lamp on the small desk in the guest room,
Kyle remained at Tyler's bedside, working his way through

yet another of the ancient archives. Tyler continued to fight against the tug of weariness and asked Kyle questions about what he was reading to keep his mind off things. "Find anything interesting?"

"It's about the Original Mother," Kyle said under his breath as he read. "Here is this part that doesn't make any sense. Something about the eldest children…keeps coming up, but I can't quite put my finger on it. Whenever I think I'm close, the text ends or turns into those symbols, but the one who seeks truth, right?"

Tyler, intrigued now, repeats the phrase "Original Mother…seek truth," an idea ignited. "Kyle, I need the journal from the study. There might be something in there that I missed."

With a nod, Kyle set the book aside.

"Of course, we'll figure this out, Ty."

CHAPTER TWENTY-TWO

THE RIBBON TIES

A suffocating silence filled the room as Tyler lay in the comfort of the bed. Kyle left for the study hours ago, and each minute that ticked by gnawed at Tyler's patience. His body still ached. Every limb felt heavy, as though made of iron, but the necessity of finding answers propelled him forward. Tyler slowly rose from the bed with stiff, achy, slow movements. Using the wall to help support his weight, he started shuffling forward slowly, feeling the cool of the floor beneath his feet through the thin fabric encasing his feet.

Reaching the hall, the manor seemed to be in sleeping silence: no clatter from the kitchen, no distant voices or footsteps, just a heavy, oppressive silence in the air. As Tyler drew closer to the study, a sliver of light shone through the partly open door, pulling him toward it. Pausing at the threshold, he hesitated and leaned into the door. He could hear the low tones of a conversation behind it. "What did Tyler say he discovered in the journal?" The question, his name, and James's voice stopped him.

"It was just that he needed it." Kyle replied tensely, "James, what happens when the royal bloodline is restored?"

James responded with a measured calm. "Once the Connected Key is whole, it will revive the royal blood. Diana's visions have never been wrong."

"But if reuniting Tyler with his brother is the key, why wait?" Kyle pushed impatience, evident to Tyler's ears, through the solid door. He leaned in, heart a drummer on his ribs. James sighed, resignation traveling through that one sound.

"There is an old story about twins in the archives. Their powerful bond and willingness to protect each other are unimaginable. I've witnessed it with my children. The story tells of a tested relationship and the demise of love once shared, allowing darkness to grow." James said.

"Is it true? Could the same happen to Tyler and Rennon?" Kyle's skepticism was clear.

"We can only hope not," James replied gravely, "But now, we have no choice. The Vasilikós lineage must be resurrected—it is what our fates and Diana's rely on." As Tyler inched closer, the newly laid floorboards betrayed him with a sharp creak. Wincing at the note, Tyler froze, but it was too late. James appeared at the door, his expression a cascade of concern.

"Shouldn't you be resting, Tyler?"

"I couldn't wait any longer," Tyler murmured, embarrassed by being caught eavesdropping.

"Come in. We were just discussing the future," Kyle said, softer. Tyler followed, and his eyes shifted to the big desk. He noticed the repaired window behind it for the first time—a reminder of the threat Raven and Solomon pose.

"The twins you mentioned from the story, James—are they Aïra and Drëi?" Tyler asked. James nodded, his eyes not quite meeting Tyler's as he sat behind the wooden desk.

"Yes…how do you know those names?" Tyler considered, for a moment, telling James about the book Kyle held and its fading ink and riddles, but he didn't.

"And what happened to them—will happen to Rennon and I when we reunite?"

Unspoken fears lined James's face. "It is unsure. But the Cerif have set out to find the Connected Key. The Shafeir have been deprived of our true potential and purpose since the fall of the royals. You both will be vital to our defense to restore what was lost."

Kyle interjected sharply, "But you already consume blood, isn't that enough?"

James's expression soured as if offended by the words. "Not for true power. The blood of animals cannot sustain a Shafeir, nor could the warm-blooded being of this realm," James explained. Suspicion flickered in Tyler's eyes.

"But my blood will, won't it?"

The room fell silent. After a tense pause, Kyle spoke, his voice low. "My mother once mentioned the gifting ceremonies, how the royals bled for their guardians, but you can't do that to Tyler. He's only one person. He can't bleed for you all."

"Kyle, it's okay. Diana needs me. I'll do whatever it takes," replied Tyler. Though doubt shadowed his words, he began feeling like a tool to the Shafeir for power.

James offered a weary smile. "Thank you, Tyler. I only hope your brother agrees."

***

It was back to the comfort of bed, and Tyler was beginning to feel stronger. His limbs were responsive, awake, and obeying his commands. The expected guests still hadn't arrived, but James and the twins stayed in the bunker with Diana, just waiting beside her bed. After being at the manor for so long, Tyler finally convinced Kyle to go home for once, and he knew Kyle's mom would be ecstatic with everything that happened. The idea made Tyler wonder what kept his guardians so long to return. They were already a day late. His mind again began to retrace things—like getting the journal, which was still in the study.

Pulling himself out of bed once more was easier this time, and he found himself behind the wooden desk with the journal before him in no time. He had to know what happened with the first gifted blood twins. The further he thought of it, the journal on the desk flung open, its cover smacking hard onto the desktop as though a hidden force had somehow propelled it to a specific page within. Tyler moved to look closer as dark ink began to swirl.

Twofold become aligned in time…

A clear sign that the journal held answers. "All right, it's time I got something out of you this time," he said, studying the words before they faded from the page. "Tell me the truth about the first gifted blood twins." He commanded. There was no swirling ink this time—the minutes felt like hours until finally, the swirl began, forming an image this time: the silhouette of two people—below it, text.

Birthed as one, the two of sum, darkness cries and evil lies, create broken ties, say those of whom darkness now thrives.

More riddles. It wasn't a surprise to Tyler, but this time, the ink did not fade from the page. Tyler knew that whatever happened to the twins ended with sorrow and pain. "Who created you, who wrote in this journal?" He asked. His tone was a passive thought spoken aloud as he ran a finger along the inked page. The page opposite the image began to swirl with ink.

The first of many, the father, of none. The one who saved you, the night before we begun.

Tyler had traced his finger over the ancient text. Slowly, like morning mist at dawn, the inked glyphs clouded from the page, leaving one enigmatic symbol behind. Unlike anything he'd seen in the countless dusty journals and brittle pages of the manor's vast collection, intrigue pricked at the back of his neck. He leaned even closer, "A sign, but of what?" he murmured to himself, the breath of his worlds stirring the air, more riddles and signs. Tyler's first impulse was to show James and the others. They could know what the symbol meant, perhaps uncovering something more. But a sharp memory halted him.

The journal's messages were secret, only to be revealed to those of royal blood. Tyler snatched a notepad from the cluttered desk. He was so hurried that his hands trembled slightly as he copied down the bizarre symbol. His pencil scratched with urgency at the paper, and he finished, tearing the page free with a decisive rip. The sound was curiously loud in the silent study. He closed the book with a gentle thud and slid the piece of paper into his pocket.

His steps were soft against the floorboards as he left the study. When he finally reached the door, his hand hesitated for a moment above the knob. The sudden sound of voice filled the air. Racing through his mind about who the voices might belong to, the symbol on a scrap of paper burning a hole in his pocket and mind, and now, guests had arrived at Scotler Manor.

PART IV

CHAPTER TWENTY-THREE

ENTER NEW WORLD

As Tyler stood at the top of the grand staircase of Scotler Manor and looked toward the crowded entrance, his heart hammered against his chest. Below the glittering patterns thrown by the chandelier on the polished floors combined with the smell of fresh flowers, Cassandra stood unmistakable, her shoulder-length golden hair flowing, petite, and graceful among the gathered group. Her light musical laughter drifted to Tyler's ears, dancing with the deeper tones of Rebecca's and Rion's voices. Beside her, Tyler's attention shifted and landed on Rennon—a reflection of himself. He stood, hands buried in his simple but stylish clothing pockets. His hair was even more unruly and longer than Tyler's, giving him an added touch of effortless charm.

It was a visual jolt, almost like stepping into a dream or forgotten memory. Through Tyler's thoughts, a noise suddenly broke out as the front door was pushed open. Kyle walked in, almost running Rennon over with his hurried entrance. "Oh, sorry, Ty—" he started before stopping when his eyes shifted from Rennon's unimpressed smirk to Tyler on the staircase—realization dawning on his face, a sheepish grin overcoming his confusion.

Upstairs, Tyler's initial urge to laugh at the mix-up evaporated under the weight of all eyes suddenly on him. Heart pounding again, he descended one stair, his smirk faltering into an awkward grin. "Looks like you mistook him for me, Ky," Tyler called down, his voice echoing slightly in the spacious entry. Rebecca's squeal pierced the silenced room.

"Tyler!" she exclaimed, her voice echoing off the high ceilings as she dashed up the stairs, meeting Tyler halfway. She enveloped Tyler in a tight embrace, "I've missed you." Tyler smiled, resting in her arms, "I guess you can say we took the scenic route back," she laughed, releasing her grip on Tyler to loop her arm through his as they walked down together. Cassandra stepped forward at the foot of the stairs with open arms and a warm, welcoming smile.

"You do look so much like your father. Just like Ren," she said. Tyler hesitated, then returned her embrace, his eyes still on Rennon, who watched him with the same unreadable expression.

"I'm sure you know who this is," Rebecca said.

His smirk was a challenge.

"Hey," he greeted.

"Hi," Tyler replied.

The word hanging awkwardly between them.

Rennon was a little too familiar, verging on disturbing, for Tyler's taste. He was just too real compared to the illusion Tyler had in his mind when imagining him. "Try to keep to your head from now on, will ya?" Rennon's tone was teasing but edged with snark.

"There wasn't much in there anyway," Tyler shot back, the retort slipping out before he could stop it. Interrupting the mounting tension, Cassandra turned to the room at large.

"And where is our host? Where is James?"

"He's with Mom in the bunker," Caleb called from behind, his voice steady despite the undercurrents of concern that flickered across his face.

"A bunker?" Rennon scoffed.

"Yes, a reinforced shelter underground," Kyle said, stepping past Rennon with a glare. "Maybe your brother ought to be in that head of yours, after all, teach you a thing or two."

Tyler watched, a mix of amusement and surprise stirring within him. Kyle had never been one for snarky comments. If Rennon kept this attitude, Tyler wasn't sure they would ever be like Kodi and Caleb. As Rebecca herded the group toward the bunker, her usual maternal instincts took over. Kyle led the way, his steps determined as the others followed.

They entered the bunker into Diana's bedroom, which seemed to shrink in the presence of them all. The mood shifted palpably. They stood in silence as James knelt by Diana's bedside, her condition visibly worse than before. James seemed to be whispering in her ear. Cassandra's hand flew to her mouth as she took in the sight of her sister. James finally stood and turned. His expression was weary but composed. "Thank you all for coming. Diana is stable for now but may soon worsen if we don't do something…" His voice trailed off, heavy with fear.

"Oh, James," Cassandra cried out, embracing him.

"Wonderful to see you, sister."

Rennon stepped forward, surprising Tyler with his solemn tone. "James, how can we help Diana?" He asked. James left the room, Tyler and the others closely behind him as he approached the bookshelves near the wall of surveillance monitors.

"From what we know, we need to make the two halves of the key whole," James said, pulling a book from the shelf and laying it open on the already crowded table.

"Okay, how does that happen?" Rennon asked.

"Unfortunately, this text does not say how."

James replied.

Tyler leaned over the table, spinning the book right side up. The text was vague, a running trend of the archived text and journals. "I know where we can find answers." Tyler said, "I will be right back." As Tyler headed for the staircase, a glimpse into Diana's room weighed on him. He knew he had to tell James and the others about the hidden text if they were going to save Diana.

Tyler pushed open the heavy, secret door to the kitchen, caught off guard by what was behind it. The head chef stood behind the stone slab counter, slicing a mountain of fruits. Tyler managed a smile as the chef caught his gaze. Just nodding in response, an acknowledgment of him, speaking no word as if his appearance from behind the hidden door was no surprise. Tyler continued, turning the corner before going to the study area where the journal was, then returned to the bunker.

"The same thing happened to me before he projected into my head," Rennon's voice traveled up the staircase as Tyler descended.

"What happened to you?" He asked.

Rennon spun, gesturing to Kyle beside him. "The Alexos tells me you had a weird trip before you mind-jumped me."

Tyler looked between the two of them before nodding. "You are the Alexos, right?" Rennon taunted, turning to Kyle, but before he could respond, James interjected.

"Is that the journal I gave you?" He asked. Tyler nodded, approaching the table and placing the open book beside another.

"Yes." He replied, running a finger along the blank page. Tyler flipped page after page to the ink that remained, pointing to it.

"What is all of this?" Rennon asked.

"I don't see anything," James added.

"You can see it too? That would make sense." Tyler replied.

"The truth lies within, the one who—" Rennon said, beginning to read the page.

"I don't understand," Cassandra interjected. Tyler looked up at the confused faces.

"Sounds like ancient gibberish," Kodi added.

"So then, you can't read or hear it," Tyler murmured. Flipping the book's pages again to the strange symbol revealed to him before. "Rennon, look at this symbol." Rennon's hand touched the page, and what happened next was beyond Tyler's wildest imagination. The world around Tyler disintegrated into nothingness.

His body spasmed with pain until, all at once, there was nothing. The last thing he saw was Rennon's face, twisted in horror as he was, as everything dissolved. It was a dark void—the same darkness that Tyler was put into in the study, a trembling world around him.

Tyler: Hello?

Rennon: What's happening to me?

Tyler: Who's there?

Rennon: Tyler?

Tyler: Rennon?

Rennon: What the hell is going on? What did you do?

Tyler: I didn't do this.

Rennon: Can you see where you are?

Tyler: No. Can you?

Man 1: Do not be afraid.

Rennon: Who the hell is that?!

Tyler: Who…who's there?

Man 1: There is no time. Find the one that was lost.

Tyler & Rennon: What?

The air was electric with an unnatural stillness as the shadows retreated. Rennon's body lay at his side, still next to Tyler. Beside them stood Rebecca and Rion, whose faces were now chiseled with concern. As if coming from a distance, the voices inside Tyler's head returned, whispering symphonies that grew louder with each passing moment with the receding darkness. The sudden silence was a surprise, and then, when clarity came back, Rebecca's voice cut into the silence sharp and urgent.

"Tyler! Can you hear me?"

Tyler blinked hard against the harshness of the room's light, vision stuttering back into focus. His head felt stuffed with cotton, the remnants of another strange episode. "I can hear you. What…what just happened?" he asked. The words came out in a husky whisper, barely audible above the hum of tension that filled the room. Scanning the bunker, Tyler's eyes landed on the Scotlers—James, Cassandra, and the twins—all mid-stride, their faces blank. Rion knelt beside Rennon, who was groggily coming to, his eyes blinking open and shut in confusion. Kyle was beside Rebecca. She moved closer to him.

"We aren't entirely sure what happened. The moment you and Rennon touched that book, there was a surge, like a shockwave, and everyone just…stopped."

"Like in the study, Ty," Kyle added.

Rennon groaned, lifting his hands to the light. "My hands…" he said as Tyler looked over again. His skin was marked with intricate symbols, glowing faintly before beginning to fade. Tyler quickly raised his own to find the same markings on his skin. He traced the lines, fascinated until the symbols dissipated like the ink of the journal.

"Woah…" he murmured, to himself.

"What's wrong?" Rebecca asked, squinting at Tyler's now unmarked hands. "What are you two seeing?" It was then Cassandra stepped forward—her trance seemingly broken. With a solemn grace, she lowered her head, kneeling with a hand over her chest.

"The Shafeir are here to serve the royals, those with gifted blood," she said in devotion. James and the twins did the same; their faces were stern. They bowed and knelt, hands crossed over their hearts in a sign of loyalty or perhaps fear. The room filled with silence as Tyler processed the moment and the Shafeir's declaration.

CHAPTER TWENTY-FOUR
THE TRAINED EYE

Dawn was breaking, but light fell too gently on the massive study window as Tyler looked beyond thoughtfully. Another misty morning, dewy—time for tranquility when the world is stillness wrapped in silence. Wisps of clouds tumbled lazily off the towering trees that guarded the manor, their slow, steady movement mirroring the brew within Tyler. A storm of emotions churned, unresolved and bitter, as thoughts of the haunting voice from the bunker mingled like a song on repeat. The voice's directive echoed chillingly: *Find the one that was lost...*

Tyler sensed that there would never be an end to the

discoveries he would make. While Rennon seemed to easily navigate this strange world, too much confidence gone a long way. Now, like some chronic itch—the mix of anger, sadness, frustration, and maybe jealousy—the truths of their reality had been given to Rennon, which Cassandra had given him. A gift to digest and reason it all. Lost in his thoughts, Tyler took the crumpled paper from his pocket and spread it open to reveal the strange mark again.

"Prince," a soft voice interrupted.

Tyler spun around to find Cassandra standing at the doorway, her words a reminder of the declaration of the Shafeir and the burden of his newfound title. "Please, I told you before, just use our names," Tyler replied, the thought of such a title sitting uncomfortably with him like an ill-fitted shoe.

"James would like to speak with you and Prin—Rennon." Cassandra corrected herself with a small nod.

"Has he found something?" Tyler's voice held traces of worry as he returned to the window, seeking the calm of the gray skies.

"We hope so. Diana doesn't have much time," Cassandra

added. Nodding, Tyler met her gaze, preparing himself for what he and Rennon may need to do to save Diana.

*

Tyler descended the stairs of the confined bunker, the air thick with anticipation as James's voice carried through the space, "We need to think about our plan."

"What are we doing to help Diana?" Tyler asked, stepping into the room where James stood at the center. Rebecca, Rion, and the twins sat scattered in chairs, their expressions tense.

"Prin—" James began, spinning to Tyler as he slowly shook his head, silencing the word about to spill from James's lips, dodging the ill-fitted title. Rebecca, Rion, and Kyle seemed unaffected by the strangeness that affected the Scotlers, charging the room's atmosphere. "Now that you and Rennon are together, the awakening can take place," James continued firmly.

"What does that mean exactly?" Tyler pressed, his tone

demanding clarity.

Cassandra stepped forward, eyes searching James's before admitting, "We aren't exactly sure how it is performed."

"But we suspect the journal might have answers," James added, just as a snapping crouch echoed through the room from the staircase. Kyle descended the stairs, biting from a green apple.

"What then?" He asked casually despite the gravity of the situation. Kyle leaned with the back against the wall, taking another bite of the apple.

"It is said in the Book of Firsts that the royal bloodline is the key to peace and balance," James replied, meeting Kyle's look.

"What book?" Tyler asked.

"There are many copies, though only one is true. The story of our ancestors, The Firsts."

"Where is the book? Do you have one here?" Tyler continued. James shook his head.

"There is a copy in Italy. I've read it," Caleb interjected.

"Another book, huh?" Kyle said dryly. Tyler met his eyes

as he chewed another piece of the apple. There was clear sarcasm in his voice, and Tyler knew why. He, too, was beginning to wonder why there were no clear answers, and all questions led to more books and journals.

"What kind of book? Can we get another?" Tyler asked.

"Not in this realm," Cassandra replied. She locked her gaze onto Tyler as she spoke.

"What does that mean?" Tyler pressed.

"Casi," Rebecca and James exclaimed in unison. The charge in the air soon turned into palpable tension as the room fell silent.

"What is it? Just tell us, now," Tyler demanded, frustration bleeding into his voice.

"He should know," Cassandra conceded, her voice resolute.

"Yes, we should both know," Rennon's voice broke through as he descended the staircase, his demeanor nonchalant. Tyler spun to face him with a nod.

"Agreed," Tyler spat, his patience wearing thin. James cleared his throat, seemingly preparing to divulge the secret.

"Yes, you should both know." He started.

"Then we order you to tell us," Rennon snapped.

Tyler paused, a frown creasing his brow.

Tyler: Can we do that?

Rennon: We are royalty, the royal twins. Of course, we can.

It was still quite unsettling for Tyler to know someone else could answer his inner thoughts. Rennon was much more comfortable in his royal role than he was, confident that he knew what he was doing. "Very well," James replied. "This world…the place we sit this very minute is—"

"A Mirror Realm," Rebecca interjected. "You should both hear this from me." She said, looking between Tyler and Rennon.

"A mirror, what?" Tyler asked.

"Mirror Realm, worlds created in mirror image to other places far from here for protection…at least, that is what we were told."

Rennon: Prison.

Tyler heard Rennon's thoughts loud and clear.

Tyler: Did you know about this?

Rennon shook his head.

"So, what are you saying? This world, my home, is fake?" Tyler asked.

"According to whom?" Rennon snapped again.

"Stories of The Firsts," Caleb answered. Tyler and Kyle exchanged a quick glance after seeing that phrase in the hidden texts—the stories and riddles beginning to make sense for Tyler.

Rennon: You know something? Tell me.

Tyler: Later.

"A haven created in the image of a world visited by our ancestors," James added.

Rennon: We are chosen. They can't keep lying to us.

Tyler: I agree.

"That's news to me, not sure I'm buying it. Scientifically speaking." Kyle said, chewing another bite of the apple. Tyler couldn't help but agree with his statement; he wasn't sure about many things, but where he lived his entire life was his home. Not a Mirror Realm created by some all-powerful ancestor to protect him.

Rennon: The question is, when did we come here?

Tyler followed Rennon's intrusive thought of questioning, "How long have we been in this Mirror Realm?" He asked aloud. Rebecca reached for Tyler's hand, pulling him close to her.

"Listen, both of you. Your parents knew the Mirror Realms would be the best place for you to live safely. Time works differently in these realms; I mean that outside of them, time moves much faster."

"How much faster?" Rennon asked.

"Two centuries? Maybe more, none of us have left the Mirror Realms since the downfall of the royal kingdom—when Aiden and Alina died." Rebecca replied.

"You can't be serious," Rennon continued.

Tyler thought his head might explode. Suddenly, his world was shrinking and becoming more expansive at the same time. Two centuries? He couldn't fathom the possibility that his parents had been dead that long. "Then, technically speaking, we're all—" Kyle started.

"Very old," Rebecca answered.

"And you know how much I admire an older woman," Rion said, stepping behind Rebecca with a wink and gentle hand on her shoulder. The joke lightened the tension in the room, but Tyler couldn't escape the shake of his reality.

Tyler: Should we tell them what that weird voice said?

When he didn't get an immediate answer to his mental question right away, Tyler shifted his gaze to Rennon. His arms were tightly crossed and his head low, shaking slightly in silence.

Rennon: Not a chance. I don't trust any of them.

"Cassandra was right for telling you all she did, Rennon. I wish I dared to do the same for Tyler, but what's done is done. You both are entering something none of us could ever understand, but know this: we are all here to help, support, protect, and love you." Tyler wrapped Rebecca into an embrace as the emotion in her voice swelled. His uncle, Rion, joined in on the moment. For that moment, Tyler settled in the comfort of his guardians, unmoved by the weight that continued to pile on him. But moments fade, as this one did.

The more time passed, the more Tyler's true feelings began to bubble to the surface. Yes, he was angry, hurt, confused, and maybe a little jealous of his brother's relationship with Cassandra as well as his knowledge of this expansive world they were part of. But maybe Rennon was right. Trust was not something he could do at the moment. Who was on their side, and were they protecting them or intent on using him and Rennon as blood bags?

CHAPTER TWENTY-FIVE
THE LOOKING GLASS

No one seemed to question it; the demand was more than enough for answers on how the awakening would be done. James and the others searched the files in the bunker, completely untouched, for any reference to the awakening ceremony. The manor had settled into a tranquil lull, punctuated by rustling pages and the occasional thump of an ancient book from the shelves in the study, where Rennon and the Scotler twins continued the search. The others were quiet in their searching, one page at a time, while Tyler sat with the journal open before him, slowly turning each page in hopes that the swirling ink might reappear. The scene in the bunker reminded Tyler of the study hall he and Kyle once worked in, where they scoured the internet and the school library to get information for their reports. Kyle turned to the internet even now for snippets of knowledge, still convinced that the reality of the Mirror Realms was a lie.

Rennon: Do you miss it?

Tyler looked up from the journal. His thoughts momentarily pulled away from his task.

Tyler: Yeah, sometimes. I still plan on going back to school.

Rennon: Casi taught me everything from books and travel.

Tyler: It was its moments. How's the search going up there?

Rennon: Join us.

"I'm going to the study for more books," Tyler announced. His voice echoed in the room. James, Cassandra, and Rebecca glanced up from their respective piles of ancient books and journals.

"All right, Tyler. Keep us posted, and on your way there, wake your uncle. I'm sure he's dozed off by now." Rebecca answered, inclining her head in a knowing smile. Tyler smiled, the seed of doubt sown by Rennon now starting to take root.

Considering how much had been hidden from Tyler over the years. Could he trust any of them? He went up the stairs to the kitchen, the moonlight shining through the rear windows, covering the room in its celestial shine, light that seemed to hold the secrets of the universe. A sudden thud on the other side of the archway broke the stillness of the scene.

Tyler entered the room to find his uncle extended on the long couch, at peaceful rest, an open book at his feet. Tyler's heart softened at the sight as memories rushed in from simpler times: they, Rion, and Rebecca could be found awake, waiting with excitement for meteor showers, as Rion would entertain them with tales of his exploits in the skies flying various planes. Not wanting to disturb his uncle, Tyler shifted his legs around on the couch and placed the book on a small table beside the sofa before continuing to study.

As he reached the door to the study, he could hear laughter and chatter coming through it; hesitating for a second, he pushed open the door to feel life, light, and warmth within the room, more so than down in the bunker. "What's everyone laughing at?" Tyler queried as he sat between Caleb and

Kodi. They both laughed in reply. Rennon slammed a book shut at the bookshelf and sat behind the wooden desk.

"You two can hear each other, right?" Caleb asked as if the question were a challenge.

Rennon: It's all right. They understand.

"We can," Tyler answered hesitantly.

"Don't ever fight it. It only makes things difficult," Kodi added. It was clear he spoke from experience.

"There are other benefits to our mental connection apparently," Rennon said, "they showed me, Tyler. I can show you." Intrigued, Tyler stood, joining Rennon at the desk. Rennon closed his eyes, and Tyler sat before him, doing the same. He focused on their connection, and within moments, Tyler was transported back to the dark space. A glimmer of light brought forth a vivid scene—an ancient castle by a roaring sea, the details as crisp as reality.

He and Rennon stood amongst civilians of the kingdom as changing images and sounds swirled around them—Cassandra's voice weaving through the noise.

Rennon: I dreamt of this place every night as a kid.

Tyler marveled at the details around him, the faint smell of salty seawater and the distant waves crashing against the shoreline. The voice of Cassandra telling a young Rennon a bedtime story grew louder. The scene began to change, sounds of war, panic, and destruction, each distinct to Tyler's ears as if they were being downloaded to his memory.

Tyler: So, we can share more than our thoughts.

Rennon: The connection we share is more than we thought.

"How?" Tyler gasped, the vision faded, returning to the study.

"Think of your minds as an infinite room with several walls. You choose which walls come down and open for the other," Caleb answered.

"Feels like we were there for hours," Tyler uttered.

"Only a few minutes outside of that connection," Kodi replied. Tyler was shocked. The vision felt like hours, and the vivid emotions, days. Tyler stood from the desk and went to the window he found solace in, still reeling from what he'd seen and heard.

"What about other voices? Do you hear those in your

head, too?" He asked, spinning to face Caleb and Kodi, who were still on the couch. The question puzzled them as they exchanged a glance.

"We don't—have you heard something?" Caleb asked.

Tyler: Do we tell them?

Rennon: Not yet. I may have found something about that.

Tyler shook his head, "and what about the castle?" He added. "Is that somewhere outside of this realm?"

"Home," Caleb said softly. His voice was barely a whisper. Tyler turned back to the window and looked up at the night sky.

"Do you know what it's like?" He asked, his gaze fixed. Before he was answered, Kyle burst into the room, his breath heavy and expression urgent. Rennon stood from the desk, as did the Scotler twins. Tyler spun from the window. "Kyle, what is it?"

"James and Rebecca think they've found something." Tyler felt a pit in his stomach instantly as he heard the news in fear of what surprise might be coming next.

*

Tyler entered the bunker first. Nearly every book on the shelves had been removed. James, Rebecca, Cassandra, and Rion stood around the table at the center of the room. Short stacks of books were scattered throughout the space. "What did you find?" Tyler asked as the group turned to him, Rennon, Kyle, and the Scotler twins.

"We didn't find it exactly," Rebecca started.

"A phrase you discovered in the study," James added.

"A riddle?" Rennon murmured, reading Tyler's thoughts.

"Correct," Cassandra answered.

"Twice, in time, twofold align. Bled blood combine. Twelve of, twelve, nine. Midnights eve divine." Tyler repeated the phrase. "What am I missing? Do you know what it means?"

"Yes. I believe this is vital to the awakening ceremony." Cassandra answered. She picked up an open book from the table and presented it to Tyler. He skimmed the page momentarily before turning it to find a page torn from its spine.

"What's missing?" Tyler asked. He also recalled the missing page from the book in the study, the thought pulling at his distrust. Were these pages being hidden intentionally? Tyler hated the idea of more secrets and lies.

"That's as far as we got," Rebecca said.

Rennon: You've been getting messages from that journal. Tell them.

Tyler: Now?

"Tyler found something, too," Rennon said as he nudged Tyler with an elbow. He reached into his pocket for the crumbled paper.

"When I asked who created the book, a symbol in the journal was revealed to me," he said, coming toward the table and spreading the paper. There was an immediate gasp in the room as James and the others examined the symbol on the paper.

"Ancient," Rebecca said.

"Firsts," James added.

"Vim," Cassandra stuttered.

"What does it mean?" Tyler asked, scanning their faces.

"It means that journal is very old, and how it came to my possession in the archives I received is a complete mystery," James replied.

"Tyler, this journal is quite possibly the Book of Vim, also known as the Book of Power. Created by our ancestors and thought to be lost after the deaths of the first Connected Key." Cassandra said, running a hand through her hair in disbelief. "Impossible."

CHAPTER TWENTY-SIX
THE BARRICADE

All eyes were enthralled on Tyler and Rennon as he sat with the open journal. "Ask it about the awakening," James said softly, his voice low. Tyler's eyes flitted between James and Rennon before settling on the journal's blank pages.

"How do I perform the awakening ceremony?" he asked.

Rennon leaned forward, his eyes narrowing in concentration on the page as Tyler's question hung in the air. The brush of Tyler's finger over the page was a gesture for the ink to answer and swirl the usual black bleeding from the page. But there was nothing for a moment; the ink did not appear. Instead, the pages of the journal remained blank as Tyler flipped furrow-browed through them. "Something's wrong. It didn't take this long before," he murmured.

"Let me try it," Rennon suggested, his voice steady. He slid the open book towards him. Tyler stood, circling behind Rennon to watch. "Tell us about the awakening ceremony," Rennon commanded. The room seemed to hold its breath, and within seconds, the familiar swirling ink began to dance across the page. "Woah," Rennon breathed out, awe coloring his tone.

Hello, Rennon Asoron.

The page greeted, the ink swirling into coherent words.

"Is it working?" Kyle asked, his eyes wide. Nods from Rennon and Tyler confirmed it.

"Let's give the princes some space," James suggested, stepping back with the others, though Tyler shot him a sidelong glance for using the title again before Rennon continued reading the message from the journal.

Two have become one, but awaken is none.

The words seemed to float between them. "How?" Tyler asked, desperate for answers.

Bled is blood that runs red—ribbons as ties where truth lies.

The book replied, its riddles deepening. Rennon met Tyler's gaze, determination settling in. "Well, you were right, Ky. We'll both need to shed blood," Tyler said.

Man 1: Find the one that was lost…

The low voice bellowed in Tyler's ears.

Rennon: That voice again.

Rennon's brow creased as he looked at Tyler.

Tyler: Who's there? What was lost?

Man 1: There is not much time.

Tyler: We need to help someone first. Tell us what to do.

Man 1: Use a blade and combine the blood.

Rennon: What?

"Do we have a blade?" Tyler asked, turning to face the group.

"A blade? For what, Ty?" Kyle's voice cracked, his concern palpable. James moved purposefully, crossing the room while mumbling the riddle.

"We have a blade," he said, opening a nearby closet.

"Tyler, I don't like this," Rebecca urged. "James told me

you know of Aïra and Drëi. I don't want to repeat that history, nor would your parents." Tyler swallowed hard, the mention of his parents striking a nerve. How would she know what they wanted? After all the secrets kept from him and lies told, now was not the time to fantasize what his parents would have wanted.

"Ty, I agree. We don't know what will happen," Kyle said.

"No one seems to know, but we can't just wait around," Rennon argued, his voice firm as he took the blade from James.

Rennon: Are we doing this?

Rennon stared decisively at Tyler. Some silent agreement between them was made when Tyler nodded. Rennon hesitated for a little bit with the blade against his hand, then let it down, placing it on the table. "What happened to the previous Connected Key?" Rennon asked.

Man 1: I can show you both.

The pages of the open book fluttered, turning until they reached the last of its pages. The swirling ink appeared again, and Tyler picked up the book, watching as words appeared.

"So, he's connected to the book," said Rennon.

"Who?" Rebecca asked. Neither answered as an image appeared on the page: the rings they wore—ancient artifacts.

Man 1: Upon performing the awakening ceremony, the Connected Key consumed with the need for power, led to their demise.

"That won't happen to us," Rennon said confidently. Tyler wished he felt the same, but it would take more reassurance than that. They had no idea what they were dealing with.

"What are you two hearing?" Rebecca asked again.

"They hear a voice," Caleb answered.

"We aren't sure," Tyler added.

"Tyler, we should try," Rennon said.

"Whatever it is, we need to prepare," Cassandra said, walking up. Although, of course, Tyler hoped he would not get too much power and lose his mind like those before him. He wanted to help Diana and, maybe, gain his own strength in the process. That, however, would not come without risk.

"If it comes to it, I'll end all of this with my talisman— draw you two back from the brink if it's the only way to keep you safe," Kyle added, holding onto the stone around his neck. Tyler felt comforted having an ally he could depend on. He knew what Kyle was capable of. Aleks would certainly stop at nothing to keep the Connected Key safe.

Tyler nodded, meeting his gaze.

"I just have one more question for this book," Tyler said, putting the book on the table again as the image faded. "What exactly is happening during the awakening?"

Man 1: That is the wrong question for the book…combining blood summons the ribbon ties, awakening the power within you both. You will either control it, or it will control you.

Tyler knew Rennon heard the voice, but neither said anything.

Tyler: Not telling them. Let's do this.

Rennon: My thoughts exactly.

CHAPTER TWENTY-SEVEN
THE MIRAGE

Tyler was spent, his body drained after too many hours awake and into the early approach of dawn, where the world was streaked with traces of night's darkness. The absolute stillness at this hour gave him a slight sense of optimism for sleep, though his body pleaded one thing: his mind was now razor-focused on preparing for the upcoming ceremony. Tyler climbed the stairs of the bunker to the kitchen, where Scotler Manor had become a transformed hollow of sounds and echoes of emptiness, a zone of dismantlement. The Scotler twins, synchronized in their movements led by Cassandra, carried the last of the furniture through the threshold of the front room as Tyler entered. Now cleared of its furnishing, the great room looked bigger somehow in its emptiness.

Tyler stood at the heart of it, taking in the space, and breathed deeply. "I will inscribe the symbols from your rings on the floor," said Cassandra as she knelt, chalk in hand. Tyler twisted the ring around his finger, eyeing the intricate carvings.

"What are these symbols exactly?"

With a knowing smile, Cassandra explained, "They are ancient—sacred to the ancestors. They might add a layer of protection for both of you." As Tyler nodded, acknowledging the plan, Rennon and James entered, with Rebecca trailing close behind.

"I wanted to see you both before everything starts." She said.

"You're not leaving, are you?" Tyler asked.

"Of course not," Rebecca was quick to reassure. "Rion and I will be down in the bunker with Diana. This will work, Tyler." Her assurance seemed to fill the room, filling Tyler's spirits. Rennon moved to stand next to Tyler at the center of the barren room, the journal in hand.

"It's time," James said, his voice carrying through the hollow room, passing the dagger to Tyler with its blade shining in the dim light and the handle cold in his palm. The room felt different suddenly, lit only by the flickering flames in the modern fireplace and the candles Cassandra had set around them. Rebecca slipped into the bunker, and Cassandra settled next to James and the twins by the mantle. Tyler caught Kyle's anxious gaze from the kitchen doorway as his foot tapped anxiously against the floor, making a slight, rhythmic tapping sound. Tyler gave a firm nod of reassurance, although the gnawing doubt in his belly stayed present.

"What now?" he whispered to Rennon.

"We shall see," Rennon replied, the journal still open in one hand as he extended the other. Tyler hesitated before bringing his eyes to the blade and then back to Rennon's waiting glance. "Well, I guess you can cut me first," Rennon offered. The reality of the situation hit Tyler: this was happening. He cautiously placed his palm behind Rennon's offered hand, carefully positioning the blade into place. He drew the blade across the skin with careful motion, a neat line forming in its wake that quickly welled with blood.

Rennon didn't flinch; his eyes were locked on Tyler's. The cut was clean and beginning to drip. Tyler swallowed hard as Kyle was immediately at his side with a towel from the kitchen.

"Thanks," Tyler mumbled, wiping the blade clean. "My turn," he said quickly, not wanting to let the nerves build again. Tyler pressed the blade to his hand, almost frantically, wincing as the sharp sting gave way to a burn. The two held their bleeding fists, joining hands. But nothing happened. A moment's pause fell over the room, the calm before the storm. "I don't feel a—" The silence shattered, replaced by an erupting rush of pain in Tyler that tore through him, his wails in harmony with Rennon's as the earth itself shook beneath their feet.

"What's going on?" Kyle yelled over a tornado's howl, now spinning in the room. The glyphs on the floor burst into bright radiance. Tyler let the blade fall; his grip on Rennon had not broken, even as agony seared through his body. The air in the room thickened as if infused with the storm itself. Bright threads of blood-red light energy danced like serpents around their clasped hands, sending spirals of writhing light and shadow up their arms.

"The ribbon ties!" James shrieked, barely audible over the howling gales of the storm, the chaotic forces drowning out everything around them. It was hard to hear anything now and difficult to see through the occasional crashing waves of power that rolled over Tyler, his senses swimming in the choreographed ritual. He only saw the hint of Cassandra, held back by the twins. Her features contorted in a feral snarl.

"What does this mean? Is this supposed to happen?" Kyle's voice rose in panic.

"The ribbons symbolize the blood gift. It must guide the flow of power," James replied.

Cassandra roared with a primal hunger, "James!" she shouted as she lunged towards Tyler. "The blood!" she spat. James tackled Cassandra, pinning her to the ground as the twins restrained her at each side again.

"Kyle, protect them!" James shouted.

"Dad, something feels wrong, the thirst," Caleb urged.

Then it started to quiet, the unnatural light fading. Tyler and Rennon stood there, separated, looking at each other wide-eyed in disbelief at what they had just done. Tyler's eyes trailed around the room; a crying Cassandra snapped free of James' hold and lunged again. Tyler threw his hand up, his head still swimming from the flare of energy, and an ethereal voice boomed throughout the space.

Man 2: BEHAVE BEFORE ROYAL BLOOD, SHAFEIR.

A brilliant flash of energy released from Tyler's hand accompanied the booming voice that sent Cassandra hurtling across the room several feet, quickly crushing her against the fireplace wall. The explosive force reverberated through the windows surrounding them, shattering them instantly. Tyler only looked at his hand, dumbfounded by what he—or the voice—had done when Kyle was suddenly there, pulling him and Rennon to their feet. "What happened to us?" Rennon breathed, his eyes darting to his now unharmed palm.

"I think it worked," Tyler replied, but his voice held a note of uncertainty that mirrored the stunned silence of the room. "But, that voice, it was different. What was that?"

"I'm not sure, but Ty, your eyes," Kyle said, a slight tremble in his voice, "were glowing…blue." He added.

Tyler blinked several times. "It happened so fast."

Rebecca burst into the room from the bunker, her eyes scanning the scene. "Is everyone okay?" she asked, her eyes darting between James and the twins, still restraining Cassandra, who recovered quickly from the blast—bloodlust in her eyes.

"We're fine," Tyler managed, the adrenaline leaving a trail of exhaustion as Rebecca rushed to his side. "Just a little shaken up."

"Our apologies," James knelt on his knee, "I take full responsibility for our reaction. I did not consider the risk we may pose."

"Cassandra could have killed him!" Kyle snapped. James lowered his gaze.

"As Shafeir hybrids, we are at our most powerful when the blood of the gifted runs through our veins—royal blood— when the awakening occurred, so had our desire for power.

You must understand. It's been a very long time since we had our full strength."

Tyler's fears were realized. The Shafeir thirsted for his and Rennon's blood, which was the true intent. But he could see in Rebecca's eyes the sense of relief cascading over her features. Tyler glanced over the faces of the Scotler twins to see a mixture of fear and disbelief—obviously, the hunger on both their parts had taken them by surprise. "We will keep our distance for now. The awakening has changed us all," James added.

"Come down to the bunker, all three of you," Rebecca urged, "James, call someone to clean up this mess."

"Cassandra will be dealt with first for her display."

He replied.

"You pass judgment on me, brother?" Cassandra snarled.

"You have forgotten our laws. We do not bear fangs before the royal blood." James snapped as Cassandra huffed, turning away.

"Laws? What laws?"

Tyler asked, not recalling learning them.

"Do not bear fangs. Protection above all. Only kill threats

to the royal family." James said, his voice even and steady.

"But what will you do to her?" Rennon asked.

James remained silent, glancing back at Cassandra but offering no solace to Rennon or Tyler before Rebecca pulled on their arms. "To the bunker, now."

CHAPTER TWENTY-EIGHT
THE CLEARING

There was no going back. The awakening reshaped Tyler's being. As ancient power now coursed through his veins, he felt a connection to something beyond himself—pain and resilience—awakening a fire within him. Yet there remained an ill-fitted feeling in all this new strength. There was an unsettling sensation of being an intruder in his fate. "How are you feeling?" Rennon asked as he sat across Tyler at the stone dining table. The question made Tyler pause, wondering if his thoughts rattled around in his head loud enough for Rennon to hear him.

"Honestly, kinda weird," he admitted, frowning slightly.

"Yeah, me too—but also—strong," Rennon said, leaning back in his chair, the wooden chair creaking slightly under his movement.

"There was so much pain before, I wasn't sure if we'd—"

"But we did survive. We were always meant to," Rennon interjected with a firm nod, his voice a comforting balm to Tyler's doubts. He knew Rennon was right, but the reality of what lay before them still jarred him. In an instant, he saw everything differently, and his home seemed to be a strange land seen through new eyes. *Home.* The very word felt alien. Was this place still his to claim? His thoughts would not be free of doubt, and they called him to some distant, unknown realm that tugged at the strings of his very soul.

Rennon: I can feel your heart racing. Take a breath. We're in this together now.

Tyler nodded, managing a soft smile.

Tyler: Thank you, brother.

Kyle entered the room from the remnants of the trashed front room. "What are you two going on about? Something wrong?" He asked, dropping into the chair opposite Tyler.

"It's this new reality that is our lives now," Tyler replied, his voice low. He glanced at Kyle, sensing his unease about the transformation his and Rennon's relationship had taken. For years, Kyle had been like a brother to him; now, the blood bond between him and Rennon added a complex layer to their dynamic.

"Yeah, I know what you mean," Kyle mumbled, eyes falling to the table. "Do you want me to take that down?" Kyle pointed to the glass of dark red liquid, which sat forebodingly on the table. He and Rennon turned to the glass, then at the reopened wounds on their palms.

"Yes, before we pass out from excessive blood loss," Rennon remarked dryly. Kyle grabbed the glass and headed toward the concealed door leading to the bunker. Cassandra's distant cries echoed as it swung open, chilling the air. "What are they doing to her?" Rennon couldn't help but blurt out, stiffened, the sound of Cassandra's agony slicing through the air.

"They won't hurt her. Not if we have anything to say about it," Tyler said in a determined voice as he hurried ahead down the stairs. The cries stopped the very second they reached the bottom of the staircase, and now the silence seemed to hang in the air heavier than before. He looked around the vast area. "James? Rebecca? Anyone?"

"In here," Rebecca's whisper drifted, inarticulate, through the closed door of Diana's room. Tyler pushed through the door to find James on his knees beside Diana's bed.

"What's wrong? Where is Cassandra?"

Rennon demanded.

"What have you done to her?" Tyler added, his voice echoing the somber atmosphere.

"Cassandra has been detained in another room, specially built to hold Shafeir," James replied, rising to his feet with a stern look.

"James, we have our blood for Diana," Tyler said as Kyle entered with the glass.

"No, wait, Kyle," Rebecca interjected quickly, "just a syringe full. Take the rest back upstairs." Rebecca drew the proper amount into a syringe. James just nodded sadly, not stopping her. She stood beside the IV bag with Diana and pushed the contents of the syringe in. "Should be any minute now," she whispered as she backed away. Again, the silence in the room was deafening as anticipation and fear mingled. Was it too late? Tyler glanced at Kodi and then Caleb, their apprehension reflecting his own.

"She can't be—" Caleb began.

"Not dead, not yet." Kodi cut in, his voice strained.

Time seemed to stretch impossibly long as they waited for some sign of change within Diana. Even with all the power that now felt available to Tyler, doubts were still nibbling at him. Why was his royal blood not working? What had they missed? More answers were needed.

Tyler: The Book of Vim.

"On it," Rennon said, responding to Tyler's thoughts aloud. Picking up on his cue, without a word, they rushed back up the stairs, Kyle trailing them. Rennon retrieved the ancient journal from the kitchen, flipping it open to a blank page.

"What are you thinking?" Kyle asked, his tone tense as he watched Rennon.

"It's time we got some straight answers from this book," Tyler declared, his determination setting in. Rennon flipped the pages of the journal a few more times, setting it back on the table.

"How are you going to do that?" Kyle asked.

"We're in control, right? This book should answer to us." Rennon answered.

"Kyle, what did your parents tell you about the gifting ceremonies, exactly?" Tyler asked.

Kyle thought for a second before answering. "Uh, just that when the royals were gifting to the masses of Shafeir, it required a lot of bloodshed and strength." He replied.

Tyler cocked his head at the answer.

"Fair enough—but we only need to do this for Diana," Tyler added. Rennon and Kyle nodded as Tyler placed his palms on the open pages, recalling the strange symbols that had once danced across his and Rennon's skin. Closing his eyes, he commanded, "Show me the gifting ceremony." This time, the book responded without hesitation. An answer hadn't written itself onto the page in swirling ink but directly into his mind—an image bursting with color and vibrancy—accompanied by a searing pain that was intense but brief, more bearable than last. Then Tyler watched the swirling ink within the darkness of his sealed eyelids clearing in seconds. Another electric shock of pain exploded as Tyler opened his eyes—his vision was clear.

"Tyler, what is it?" Kyle asked.

"I saw something, some fruit, blood-like and glowing. I don't understand it." The image in Tyler's mind faded like the ink on the page of the journal. "That was different."

"Fruit?" Rennon questioned, eyebrow raised in disbelief.

Tyler shrugged, just as baffled. "It looked like a peach, but not exactly," Tyler added. Kyle moved to the kitchen's cabinets, opening each in search of something.

"What is it, Professor Huntington?" Tyler joked.

"Let's find something like a peach," he replied, continuing his search. Tyler and Rennon reluctantly joined him, searching nearly every cabinet in the massive kitchen. For a moment, Tyler wished James hadn't dismissed the kitchen staff before the ceremony; their direction was needed now. Tyler went to the fridges—of course, there were two—and opened the first. Scanning the fully stocked shelves for fruit. Recalling the apple Kyle had eaten before, but there were none.

Only rows of juices, pre-made meals, and desserts. Impossible. He went to the next fridge and opened its doors, revealing stocked shelves for fresh fruits, vegetables, meat, and cheeses. He quickly picked a container of ripe fruit. Peaches, pears, apples, and purple plums. "Found some!" he shouted, pulling two peaches from the bunch. Tyler kicked the refrigerator doors shut with his foot as he spun to the countertop behind him.

"Okay, literal peaches. Now what?" Rennon asked.

Tyler eyed the fruit, pondering. "Ask the professor."

"Well, what else did you see?" Kyle asked, sitting in a chair at the counter. "We have a test subject. Describe what you saw, and maybe we can try replicating it somehow."

Tyler took a breath, closing his eyes to visualize the object. "The fruit was shaped just like this, but it looked different, changed somehow. Clear, and it's core—" Tyler described.

"What?" Rennon interjected, scratching his head.

"I know how it sounds, but I think anything is possible now, right?" Tyler said.

*

At least An hour passed, and Tyler had yet to decide on the fruit. Time had become a cauldron since he first set foot in the manor, and it wasn't a luxury they could afford now. Kyle pulled two more peaches, an apple, and a pear from the stock after Tyler tried eating the first in hopes that it would trigger a reaction in his mind—it didn't. The second was crushed in Rennon's hand. Still, nothing happened, no change like the one Tyler saw in his head. "Rennon, try another one," Tyler said, placing the pear from Kyle's harvest before him—the third attempt.

"I don't know what else to do," Rennon said, taking the fruit.

"Maybe try cutting it up?" Kyle said sarcastically, but the idea was intriguing.

"We should." Tyler concurred, searching the drawers

of the countertop for a knife. Finding one next to a cutting board, he pulled both out and placed them on the counter.

"Wait, that's a huge knife," Rennon said.

"It's what we have," Tyler replied. Rennon sighed, picking up the knife, and hesitantly placed the fruit on the cutting board. He began slicing the fruit.

"I don't know what this—" Either it was their collective sleep deprivation, the necessity of saving Diana, or Rennon was right about the size of a knife. But as Tyler watched the sliced fruit hit the board, the knife Rennon held slipped, landing on his finger. He cried out instantly. "I knew this knife was too damn big!" he yelled, gripping his cut finger with his hand.

"Okay, bad idea. How bad is it?" Tyler asked. He quickly pulled a hanging towel from the wall behind him, handing it to Rennon to press against his wound.

"I'll live, thanks. I've had worse." Rennon replied.

Tyler grabbed the knife and cutting board back from Rennon, cursing his failed attempt, resulting in Rennon's hand being cut again. As he placed the board and pieces of fruit in the sink, he noticed a slight squelch of Rennon's blood on a piece. Picking up the small piece of fruit to examine it, he wondered if blood was the key.

To his amazement, the fruit began to change form before his eyes. The fleshy interior was becoming a crystal clear, transparent membrane—like a fractured ice cube in water. "Rennon, you're a genius," Tyler said as he spun to face Kyle and Rennon with the fruit. "This is exactly what I saw in the vision—the fruit transformed, clear as crystal but with the core still vividly red." Tyler put the fruit in his palm, holding it out for them to see. The revelation was thick in the air: Perhaps blood could be the catalyst they'd been after. The surface of the fruit glistened, shimmering like something from space, and as Rennon and Kyle came up to look closer, their faces were in awe.

Rennon continued nursing his injured finger, leaning closer. "It's bizarre."

Ever the skeptic, Kyle wrinkled his nose as he peered at it. "Kind of like a science experiment gone wrong," he said, but his tone betrayed his fascination. Tyler turned the fruit in his hand, examining it from all angles. The kitchen's lights played across its surface, highlighting the intricate details of its altered structure.

"It can't just be the looks," Tyler said thoughtfully. "It has to be something else in our blood to cause this." Rennon agreed as he peered down at his wound.

"Maybe it's like space radiation, you know? Blood is considered the life force; maybe that causes the transformation. It might be the key part of the gifting ceremony. The power isn't in just the ritual itself, but in what we choose to sacrifice of ourselves to others." Rennon's insightful thought took Tyler aback. Kyle sighed, taking the fruit from Tyler's hand.

"So, what now? Do you start bleeding on all the fruit in the manor?" Kyle joked.

"Unnecessary," Tyler said with a slight smile tugging at the corner of his lips. "We needed to know how. Now, we do. Our blood, combined with the ceremonial intent, activates the power within. This may be all we need to save Diana," he added.

Rennon, still holding the towel against his finger, exchanged a glance with Kyle. "Let's prepare for the ceremony then," Rennon said. "We might not fully understand it yet, but we have a better idea now. We need to act while we can." Tyler agreed with Rennon.

"We'll use the peaches then." He declared.

*

Tyler did not waste a second gathering more peaches from the stock. He then pulled another one of the smaller knives from a drawer. "This has to work," he said, holding the fruit in one hand and the knife in the other. He cut off the top of the fruit and pulled it off like a bottle cap, dropping it on the counter. Next his hand, pressing the blade into his palm, the brief re-emergence of memories he had from the awakening ceremony sneaking up on him. He forced back the now swelling anticipation and made a quick cut.

The pain flared to life, turning red, and blood quickly began to pool in his hand. He held the open fruit under it, turning his wound over. It was nothing compared to everything else he had been through in the past day. Tyler palmed the fruit, lifting it from the counter as his blood steamed, hitting the countertop in small splatters. He watched hard for the change, as he'd seen before. "Should I do anything else?" he asked.

"I didn't," Rennon replied, but suddenly a faint voice flowed through the air.

Man 2: FIRST, WERE THE SEEDS SOWN…

The voice was familiar to Tyler's ears, the same tone from the awakening. It was said lightning never struck the same place twice, but it was a lie like most things Tyler was told. The bolt was explosive, all-consuming as Tyler's body seized; his arm turned wrist-up with the fruit still in hand, but it wasn't pain he felt this time. It was power.

Man 2: BOUNDLESS…BY—VIM…

"What is that voice?!" Kyle shouted as the voice swelled.

"It's the same one from the ceremony!" Rennon replied. Tyler felt the surge throughout his body, his gaze falling on his hand, which was radiating with light.

"I got this!" Tyler gritted through his teeth, enduring the

pain until the surge finally dwindled, leaving behind a pulsing sensation.

"Tyler, your eyes again," Kyle exclaimed.

Man 2: A DIRE OMEN, YET A GIFT…

Tyler: What is happening to me?

Man 2: THE DIVINE FRUIT IS TIED.

As the voice echoed its last words, Tyler felt another surge, this time from the wound in his hand. The ribbon-like threads winded over his hand and the fruit until suddenly dissipating with a bright flash. "This is it," Tyler said with heavy breath. He held in his palm the glass-like fruit he saw in his mind. Its clarity and the vivid red core almost glow under the lights. It's once fleshy nectar as clear as ice and visible to the core, which once housed a solid seed, now permeated with a blood-red liquid center.

"You did it," Rennon said, reaching for the fruit.

"We did it." Tyler corrected. Wiping his forehead, cold sweat mixed with a sense of triumph as he stumbled back from the countertop. "We need to get this to James."

CHAPTER TWENTY-NINE
THE FIRSTS

Kyle grabbed the essentials—water and some bandages for Tyler's hand. Tyler was still enamored by the profound transformation of the fruit. Low groans and creeks from the hidden metal door rang through the kitchen as Rion poked his head in with a concerned look. "You three all right?" Rion's voice cut through Tyler's dazed state. First, his head appeared from behind the door, and then he pushed the door far enough wide to slip through.

"You're just in time, Uncle Rion," Tyler murmured, his voice a mixture of exhaustion and relief. Rennon spun around, the fruit still in his palm.

"This is what Diana needs," he said, holding the fruit up like a prized jewel. Rion crossed the room, looking shocked and worried.

"Right, okay. Probably best if I take it down since I'm not special like you all." He murmured as he looked at the palm of Rennon's hand. Tyler could hear the humor in Rion's words, but his weakness still held him. All he could do was smile as the fruit was passed to Rion.

"You're special to me, uncle," he choked out, his voice barely above a whisper. "You both should go down with him. I don't think I can move much right now," Tyler added, watching Rion's retreat through the door. Kyle looked up from bandaging Tyler's hand, exchanging a glance with Rennon.

"No way. We're going down together," Kyle said firmly.

"How's your hand?" Rennon asked, nodding towards Tyler's bandage.

"I'll live. I've had worse," Tyler replied, mimicking Rennon's earlier reassurance. A weak chuckle escaped his lips, and Kyle moved beside him, offering his shoulder as support to help Tyler stand. Together, they descended slowly to the bunker. Tyler's steps were measured and deliberate, and his mind was fixed on seeing Diana awake despite every protest of his body.

"You both probably need some food," Kyle said as they reached the bottom of the staircase. The moment Kyle mentioned eating, the hunger pang struck Tyler hard. It seemed the weakness had brought an extreme hunger with it. But there was no way Tyler could eat now.

"Later," he replied, his voice still strained. Rebecca was first out of Diana's room.

"I'm sorry, Tyler. I wish I could've been up there with you both," she said softly, embracing him. Tyler shook his head, returning her gentle embrace.

"No, we needed to do this alone," he insisted. Rion joined them, his arms enveloping Rebecca and Tyler, the fruit still secure in his grasp.

"Come in, all of you. I think James is almost ready." Rebecca said, pulling back as they entered Diana's room. The air was thick with tension. Standing beside Diana's bed, James held a large mortar bowl. Rion gave the fruit to him and stepped aside.

"Thank you all for doing this. Tyler, are you okay?" James asked, his eyes scanning Tyler's face. Tyler nodded, trying desperately to shake off the last of the haziness. James's gaze then shifted to the Scotler twins. "You two should probably step outside for this. The Tied Fruit is quite—alluring." The words of the voice returned to Tyler: *THE DIVINE FRUIT IS TIED.*

"No way. We're staying," Kodi snapped, his tone sharp but filled with sincerity.

James sighed, resigning. "Very well."

"Are you sure? I can go with you," Tyler offered, hoping to ease their discomfort.

"No, we're staying. Even if the hunger the gifted blood brings is like fire in our throats—she's worth every second of it," Caleb replied, his arm tightening around Kodi. James nodded to them both, then began grinding the pestle against the fruit, crushing it and releasing its potent scent into the air. Tyler found the smell was unexpectedly sweet, reminiscent of a ripe peach.

"James, hurry, I can smell it!" Cassandra's voice called

from the other room. James quickly set the bowl down, picking up the syringe.

"Now I need to inject this into the vein and, at the same time, pull the blade out," James said in a calm voice as he inserted the needle into Diana's skin and gently removed the blade that was protruding from her abdomen. "Can you take this, Rion? Make sure not to come into contact with its sharp edge," he ordered as Rion walked up and took the blade's handle, which he wrapped in a towel from a drawer close by. James did a few more injections until the bowl was emptied, then put it aside, taking Diana's hand in his. "Now we wait again," he murmured. The room turned into a tense silence, filled with only shallow breaths. Were they too late this time? Then, finally, Tyler heard it: a soft gasp and a floating whisper filled the air.

"James." With a collective exhale of breath that moved through the room like a wave, Tyler stepped forward to see Diana blink, her eyes open and glistening in their golden hue.

"Mom!" Caleb shouted.

"Diana," James whispered, tears rushing to his eyes. Suddenly, relief and pain filled the already tense room as they all witnessed James's love for his wife pouring out.

*

James planted another gentle kiss on Diana's forehead for a fifth time. In his example, a second later, the Scotler twins followed, placing the tenderest of kisses on either of Diana's cheeks. "Are you all right, my love?" came James's question again, but this time in a softer tone, eyes searching hers for any sign of pain or discomfort. She gave him a slight but natural curve at the corners of her lips, head supported by pillows.

"Truly, I am," Diana replied. Her eyes shifted to Tyler and Rennon, her golden yellow eyes unwavering on them. "Thank you, my princes," she said, her voice filled with deep gratitude. Tyler nodded, still trying to figure out how to respond to the royal title. "Prince Rennon," she added, nodding towards him, who wore a proud smile. "A lot has happened while I was in that slumber." She then looked at Kodi. "Kodi, take a few drops of the Tied Fruit to Case and bring her here, please?"

Kodi hesitated, looking for James's approval. James nodded slowly as he rose to his feet reluctantly from the bed. "It's all right," James said reassuringly to him before turning back to Diana. "How do you know this, my love?" He asked.

"I've been watching over you all from the Astral Realm," Diana explained.

"Astral Realm?" Tyler echoed with confusion.

Diana nodded. "Yes, a realm beyond this one, accessible only to the gifted by…invitation. Our ancestors took me there for protection from the darkness after I was poisoned." James moved closer to Diana as she talked, his lips brushing her forehead. Diana interlaced her hand with James's, speaking gently, "You seemed unable to hear my telepathic messages about the Astral Realm or the ancient text for Tyler."

"I see," James murmured.

"Wait, what ancient text?" Tyler interjected.

"The journal with the entry about the Tied Fruit. Though it seems you figured it out well enough," Diana replied, her eyes meeting his sparkling with pride and relief. "Tyler, you and Rennon have been—" Diana started but was interrupted as Cassandra burst into the room, followed by Kodi.

"Sister!"

Cassandra exclaimed as she went running to Diana.

"Good to see you, Casi," Diana said as Cassandra let go.

"I am—so sorry to all of you for my behavior," Cassandra said, tears welling in her eyes, her head bowed in shame. Tyler saw how embarrassed and ashamed Cassandra was, her eyes desperate for forgiveness.

"It's okay, Casi. It is my fault. I didn't know what would happen," James said, seeking forgiveness. Diana propped herself up in the bed.

"Well, now that we are all here, I have important news."

"What is it, Diana?" asked James. The stomach cramp of Tyler's hunger rose again; this time, the pangs returned worse than before, sending his head spinning slightly dizzy.

"Tyler and Rennon have been called to the Astral Realm by a First," Diana said.

"Who?" Rennon asked before Tyler could find the will.

"The First are our ancestors, our direct connection to

the Original Mothers," Diana continued. Tyler and Kyle exchanged a quick, knowing glance, their shared recollection of the knowledge coming to mind. But Tyler was starting to lose it; the weight of everything he had done affected him. "There were five. They were the first bestowed with the gifted blood. Three of the royal family…and two others turned True Vampire, the first of their kind. We must go to the Astral Realm now," Diana concluded.

PART V

CHAPTER THIRTY

ENTER NEW REALM

The thought of traveling anywhere right now made Tyler even dizzier. He needed a moment to recover. Just the idea of an ancestor wanting to meet him made his brain ache. "An ancestor there would like to meet you both. They've waited a long time for the awakening to take place to do so," Diana said. Tyler saw Rennon's eyes perk up with intrigue.

"How do we get there?" He asked.

"I can take you, but we must do it soon; my connection to that realm is not forever."

"Diana, you can't go back there. We just got you back," James said with a nudge to her shoulder. Tyler was quiet for a moment, lost in thought about the trip. He must have been thinking loud enough for Rennon to hear when he suddenly replied.

"I think we just need a little while to rest. Get some food." Tyler met Rennon's gaze.

Tyler: Thank you. I wasn't sure how to say that.

Rennon: I can feel how weak you are. You need sustenance.

"Of course," Diana agreed.

"I'm sure you could rest as well, Mom," Caleb added.

Diana turned to Caleb, smiling. "I'll be okay. I feel nearly restored, and my wound is healed. I've been in bed long enough, haven't I?"

"No surprise there. You are the strongest of us right now," Cassandra replied. Her tone was flat, a blanket of jealousy toward Diana for reaching full strength before she did, perhaps?

*

Tyler raided the fridges upstairs, grabbing anything edible in sight. Kyle was alongside him, filling the countertop with fruit, vegetables, cold-cut sandwiches, and various drinks.

"Think this is enough?" Kyle asked.

Tyler turned from the fridge, a cheese stick hanging out of his mouth, nodding. "I think so," he answered, biting the stick in half. Rennon sat at the table, eating one of the sandwiches.

"What do you think it will be like?"

Tyler chewed another piece of cheese and, with his overflowing plate of food, joined Rennon at the dining table. "I'm not sure. Never considered going to another realm before."

"I wonder if it's anything like the dreams I had as a kid," Rennon added. Tyler chewed in silence, emptying his plate. He figured he could consider the thought more seriously once his stomach was full. Kyle was on the other side of the table from Tyler, chewing on a hard-boiled egg. The others didn't seem so keen on eating. They stayed down in the bunker with Diana. Suddenly, an intrusive thought came to Tyler.

Rennon: I was thinking the same thing.

"They'll want us to make more Tied Fruit for them," Tyler said, putting his fork down.

"Did I miss something?" Kyle asked.

"Tyler and I were just wondering why no one else was eating with us. They know what the Tied Fruit did for Diana, returning her to full strength, and now they will also want their full strength," Tyler explained.

"Oh," Kyle replied.

Tyler wasn't sure he could handle making more of the Tied Fruit, even if he and Rennon did it together. It was as if his worst fears were coming true. He and Rennon would be nothing more than blood bags for the Shafeir, after all. The thought made Tyler wonder what his ancestors did when choosing to give their blood to the Shafeir in exchange for protection if that's indeed what happened. "Of course, they would want to be at their full strength. But judging from how Cassandra reacted to just the smell of our blood, I wonder how sustainable this will be. It takes a lot out of us just to create one fruit. What's enough to satiate their thirst?" Tyler added.

Man 1: Creating Tied Fruit will be easier in time.

Rennon: You again?

Tyler: Who are you?

Man 1: Visit the Astral Realm with Diana.

Rennon and Tyler locked eyes, nodded, and got up from their chairs without saying a word. They went across the room to the hidden door and down the steps. "Guessing I missed something else?" Kyle yelled from the table as they passed. Tyler was beginning to feel like his old self. And now, he couldn't wait to learn who the voice in their head was. He and Rennon descended the last steps to see James, Rebecca, Rion, and the twins sitting in the room.

Diana came from her room at that moment, patting a fresh set of clothing on herself. She appeared renewed, her eyes were bright.

"You're out of bed already?" Tyler asked.

She smiled.

"A shower and change of clothes were needed."

"We want to go to the Astral Realm." Rennon's voice was as equally eager as Tyler felt.

Tyler nodded. "We're ready."

"Very well. Shall we go upstairs?" Diana replied.

"Tyler, are you sure about this?" Rebecca asked, her voice laced with concern. She and Rion clung to one another as if holding the other back from saving Tyler. "What about school and graduation?" she added. Being swept up by everything, Tyler had nearly forgotten about graduation. He still wanted to return to school, and graduation had always been his goal; it was all he and Kyle talked about when they started their senior year.

"That's right, graduation is coming up," Tyler said, meeting Kyle's gaze as he descended the staircase.

"We could check in with the school," Rion said. "Make sure they aren't too suspicious."

"Kyle, you should go too. Make sure your mom knows what's happening and check in with the school," Tyler added. Kyle had been with him through this entire journey, and it wouldn't feel right without him, but Tyler knew how much Kyle's studies meant to him, and he couldn't ask him to give that up. Kyle shot a nod toward Rennon, then at Tyler.

"But the minute you need me, I'll activate this thing and

be here." With a quick hug from his aunt, uncle, and best friend, Tyler trailed Rennon and Diana up the steps from the bunker. James had not let Diana out of sight since she awoke, but she insisted that he, the twins, and Cassandra—still trying to control her bloodlust—keep watch over the manor while they went to the Astral Realm. They would be far too vulnerable otherwise. Diana swung the door to the bunker open into a kitchen of devastation—refrigerators raided, fruit spread over the countertops.

"Well, looks like you found something to eat," Diana said. Tyler and Rennon both apologized, but perhaps too soon, as Diana was already walking toward the front room. She jerked to a stop at its threshold. The whole room was still a disaster area from the awakening. Debris left from the explosion, walls, and floor scorched. The curtains swayed lightly from the breeze coming in through the broken windows.

"Sorry about this, too," Tyler replied. Diana ran a hand through the curls of her hair.

"Not the worst state I've seen a home of mine in. Luckily, we don't have neighbors yet," she replied calmly. "The study it is."

"We'll clean it up, promise," Tyler added.

Diana raised a hand to him, smiling. "We have more important matters to attend to. James will have this taken care of." She continued up the second staircase to the study. Once inside, Diana gestured for Tyler and Rennon to sit. "Please, the process shouldn't take long."

"What process?" Rennon asked.

"You and Tyler will sit beside me and join hands. I will do the rest," Diana said, sitting between them on the couch, taking each of their hands in hers. "Close your eyes and relax."

Rennon: Easier said than done.

Diana: Try to relax.

Tyler and Rennon shot open their eyes at each other. "My ancient artifact, this pendant necklace, gives me clairvoyant abilities. We are linked at the moment." To think that yet another person could hear his thoughts put Tyler on edge. He felt Rennon's mind relax as he did.

Diana: Good. I will take us to the Astral Realm now.

At first, there was only darkness behind Tyler's closed

eyelids. It was a familiar darkness that he found himself in with Rennon when they connected to the Book of Vim. And then, all of a sudden, a spectrum of color opened before Tyler's eyes. Diana's voice echoed in his head, dragging him into a light-filled space.

Diana: You will hear a lot—prepare your minds.

Tyler: This place—

Rennon: —is amazing.

Once the colors passed, Tyler found himself in a new place. He glanced down at his hands and body and saw them glowing with light. The world around him was as tangible as the one he left. Rennon was beside him, looking over his astral self. The only difference Tyler could see was that Rennon had large wings coming from behind him, feathers of white light, like an angel, wings that sprang from his back effortlessly, fanning the air.

Rennon: Woah, this feels different.

Diana: I know this may feel strange at first.

Rennon: This feels awesome.

Tyler: What about our bodies? How are we here?

Diana: Every gifted being has an astral form—in life and death. Notice your eyes…

Tyler and Rennon exchanged another glance, their eyes aglow with electric blue halos.

Diana: …they are activated here—a sign of your connection to royal Vasilikós lineage.

Tyler shifted his gaze back to the world again—one of light, an open field, grass-covered, warm. Off in the distance, trees seemed to glow of their own volition. Several branches bore some bizarre fruit. As he gazed upon the fruit, something seemed eerily familiar, like what he had created outside this place but not. Diana led Tyler and Rennon through the field. More materialized into view as they proceeded, including a door a thousand times the size of any other that Tyler had ever seen.

Tyler: What is that?

Diana stopped, kneeling in silence before the door.

Diana: He approaches…

Tyler: Who?

Diana: Born of blood, connected by key, divided in three—

The Firsts, the one called—

Man 2: I AM NYMBUS.

A voice bellowed around them, all familiar to Tyler. Diana kept her head bowed.

Diana: Nymbus.

Tyler looked around for the being, but there was none. Following Diana's lead, he and Rennon dropped to one knee, bowing their heads.

Nymbus: DAUGHTER. MY SONS. RISE.

Nymbus's voice continued as the doors split in two and opened before them. Tyler raised his gaze to see the spectrum of colored light again pouring out behind the doors.

Nymbus: WELCOME, TYLER AND RENNON ASO-RON.

CHAPTER THIRTY-ONE
THE FORTITUDE

A silhouette emerged from the radiant light, gradually solidifying into a towering figure draped in ethereal robes and gold, eyes like twin stars burning with intense wisdom and power.

Nymbus: MY CHILDREN, YOU HAVE COME FAR TO STAND BEFORE ME. YOUR BLOOD BINDS YOU TO THE DESTINY OF YOUR LINEAGE.

Diana knelt, head bowed, as Nymbus extended a hand toward Rennon and Tyler.

Nymbus: RISE AND APPROACH, FOR I HAVE LONG AWAITED THIS MOMENT.

Tyler felt a surge of warmth in his chest, a calling so deep that his body responded without hesitation. He stepped forward, Rennon beside him, and both moved toward Nymbus's gleaming figure. Through the luminescent haze, Tyler was staring at Nymbus's dizzying tall figure, his gold jewelry gleaming upon his metallic bronze skin, shining in the diffused light. The material of his clothes looked like silk, shining with an unearthly glow.

As the massive doors clanged shut behind him, Nymbus ceased his advance, vanishing momentarily in a brilliant flash of light. Only to return when the light subsided, his once magnificent figure transformed—now standing only a few inches taller than James, his attire simplified to a silk-like shirt and pants, yet still draped in the opulent gold jewelry.

Nymbus: THIS FORM SHOULD BE MORE COM-FORTABLE FOR YOUR SENSES.

No longer echoey, his voice was still resonant, deep, and commanding. He came forward, and though his form was no longer threatening, he was no less intense. He gathered both Tyler and Rennon into his embrace. Tyler stood frozen, spellbound by the transformation and the warm energy from Nymbus.

Nymbus: STRENGTH YOU AND RENNON HOLD WITHIN.

Nymbus continued, a smile playing upon his lips, acknowledging Tyler's astonishment.

Tyler: It was you, the voice I heard during the awakening.

Nymbus: INDEED.

Rennon: And it was your voice when we created the Tied Fruit?

Nymbus nodded. Caught up in the revelation, Tyler ventured further.

Tyler: And the book?

Nymbus shook his head in caution.

Nymbus: THE BOOK IS SOMETHING ELSE ENTIRELY—BUT BE MINDFUL OF IT.

Rennon: And who made you—our kind?

Tyler: Did you create the Book of Vim?

Nymbus: WALK WITH ME.

With a serene smile, Nymbus put an encouraging hand

on their shoulders before leading them into the vast open field that lay endlessly in front of them, with Diana trailing behind.

Nymbus: AS TO YOUR QUESTIONS…YOU MUST FIRST UNDERSTAND THE KEY.

Nymbus swept a hand mid-air, causing light particles to swirl, forming a vivid scene.

Nymbus: WE, THE FIRSTS, HOLD A COLLECTIVE POWER MEANT TO SAFEGUARD THE REALMS AND SUSTAIN PEACE. THIS POWER, SHARED WITH OUR DESCENDANTS AND THROUGH THE CONNECTED KEY, BIRTHED ANOMALIES—AÏRA AND DRÈI.

Tyler observed the scene of a colossal Nymbus amongst other figures weaving light and seeds, sprouting into beings; some gave birth, others bitten—turned into something else.

Tyler: So then, why create the book? Why share your power and not use it yourselves?

Nymbus turned, his expression grim.

Nymbus: THE POWER BESTOWED TO THE FIRSTS WAS NOT MEANT TO BE HOARDED—BUT SHARED. HOWEVER, NOT ALL BELIEVED THIS TO BE THE

PATH. THE BOOK WAS CREATED BY MY BROTHER, REMUS. HE BELIEVED THE POWER WAS BEING STOLEN FROM US. THUS, HE EMBED HIS ESSENCE INTO THE BOOK.

Tyler: So, that's what's in the book…

Nymbus: YES, THE BOOK IS A TOOL THAT MUST BE HANDLED WITH CARE.

Rennon: Who created you? Where did we all come from?

Nymbus's grin returned as he turned to the particles.

Nymbus: MOTHERS. THE ORIGINALS.

As Tyler digested this information, Nymbus waved at the illusion, ending the vision and went through the pasture. It was all becoming clear to Tyler: The Original Mothers creating the Firsts and then bestowing their power to future generations. But that one part still didn't add up. Who or what made them all? Nymbus got quiet as they walked.

Tyler: …and where did we all come from?

Nymbus: THE SOURCE IS CREATOR OF ALL.

Tyler: You gave up your power to live here alone? Do the other Firsts exist in this realm?

Nymbus: ALL WILL BE REVEALED TO YOU IN TIME. ALL THOSE WITH GIFTED BLOOD TAKE THEIR ASTRAL FORM PERMANENTLY EVENTUALLY.

Interrupted by a sudden thought, Tyler blurted out what was in his head.

Tyler: Then our parents—are they…

Nymbus: THEY RESIDE HERE, YES. IN THE KING-DOM OF LIGHT.

Rennon, catching on, pressed eagerly.

Rennon: Can we see them? Visit the Kingdom of Light?

Nymbus: YOU CANNOT. THE KINGDOM IS FOR THOSE WHO HAVE TAKEN THEIR FINAL ASTRAL FORM. YOU BOTH HAVE ANOTHER KINGDOM YOU MUST SEE TO, SHOULD YOU CHOOSE THE PATH.

A wave of disappointment washed over Tyler, dousing the flickering hope of reuniting with his parents. In all the fantastic realities he'd been faced with, this remaining hope was still just out of his grasp—even in the Astral Realm.

Nymbus: YOUR PARENTS ARE AT PEACE AND AL-WAYS WITH YOU.

Nymbus reassured them both, his voice soft as they continued under the celestial lights. The ambiance was both mystic and serene. Still reeling from the news and all he had seen so far, Tyler found the gentle touch of Diana on his back—finding some consolation in it all.

Nymbus: THERE IS SOMEONE ELSE, HOWEVER, WHO WOULD LIKE A WORD.

He gestured again with his hand, and the air whirled to life with bright particles of light coalescing in the shape of a man. The shape solidified with one blinding flash.

Man: Hello, Tyler, Rennon. Good to see you again, Diana.

The man's voice was warm and stirred memories in Tyler—hauntingly familiar, yet so out of place in this realm. Tyler made a face, concentrating now, some flicker of recognition dawning on him.

Tyler: I know you. I recognize your voice.

Nymbus: DECLAN ASORON, BROHTER OF AIDEN ASORON.

Rennon: Our uncle?

Tyler stared at Declan, recognizing their shared familial

traits—same angular facial structure, same piercing electric blue eyes. When Declan reached out a hand in greeting, Rennon jumped in first, grabbed his hand, and pulled their newly realized uncle into an eager hug.

Declan: It's nice to finally meet you both.

Tyler: But how? Are you projecting here as well?

Declan shook his head, his smile waning slightly.

Declan: No, I'm no psychic. I've taken my final astral form.

Tyler: Then how are you outside of the Kingdom of Light? I thought—

Nymbus: DECLAN'S CIRCUMSTANCES ARE— UNIQUE...

Declan smirked at Nymbus's remark but remained silent as Tyler's gaze hardened.

Declan: I gave my life many centuries ago, during the final battle with the Cerif. Your mother and father escaped that night—but the Book of Vim consumed by life, connecting me to it.

Tyler gasped softly in horror at the sacrifice.

Tyler: You died to protect us?

Rennon: I'm sorry you lost your life, uncle.

Declan: It's quite all right. My life saved many others. Now, I exist between realms.

Tyler: You were the voice telling us to find the one that was lost. What did you mean?

Declan's eyes dropped briefly, and he looked to Nymbus, who cleared his throat, obviously caught off-guard by the question.

Declan: I—

Nymbus: THOSE PART OF THE ASTRAL REALM ARE BOUND NOT TO INTERFERE WITH THE PATHS OF FUTURE GENERATIONS OF THE GIFTED BLOOD. DECLAN SHOULD NOT HAVE BEEN INTERFERING EITHER…

Nymbus gave Declan a reproachful look, and Declan lowered his head. Tyler exhaled deeply, almost audibly, frustrated. Even with learning so much, more secrets were kept from him. He wondered if the veil of mysteries and lies would ever be lifted from his family's past.

Tyler: Will this power eventually consume us, too?

The silence that followed was deafening—clearer, louder, and more precise than any answer that could have been said aloud. Nymbus gestured for Tyler to stand at his side.

Nymbus: LET US CONTINUE WALKING…IF YOU CHOOSE TO FOLLOW THE PATH OF THE CONNECT-ED KEY, YOU WILL NEED TO LEARN TO CONTROL THE POWER THE RING ON YOUR FINGERS BESTOWS YOU—BUT KNOW THAT THE CHOICE IS BOTH OF YOURS. LEARN FROM THE PAST.

The idea of more power and control had once appealed to Tyler; now, it seemed more like a deal with darkness. After everything he and Rennon had been through to get this far, Tyler wasn't sure he wanted more power. The inferno that once raged through his body while creating the Tied Fruit was enough to try and manage. Nymbus brought the group to one of the gently swaying trees they'd passed when arriving, the same tree with the fruit Tyler thought was fascinating. Nymbus plucked a single fruit from its branches. Holding it, he spoke an incantation.

Nymbus: FI—VI—DI—TIED IN THREE.

The fruit transformed, mirroring the Tied Fruit Tyler used to revive Diana.

Tyler: How did you do that? Those weren't the same words you spoke to me before…

Rennon: What do they mean?

Nymbus: THE GIFTING WILL BECOME EASIER WITH TIME. THE WORDS SPEAK TO THE THREE BOOKS CREATED MANY GENERATIONS AGO. THE BOOK OF FIRSTS, THE BOOK OF VIM, AND THE BOOK OF DIRE. ALL PARTS OF WHAT IT MEANS TO BE OF GIFTED BLOOD.

Tyler: Book of Dire?

Nymbus: ALL LIGHT MUST HAVE AN INVERSE, AN OPPOSITE.

Diana: Nymbus, it is time.

Tyler: Time for what?

Nymbus: DIANA'S CONNECTION TO THIS REALM IS COMING TO AN END.

Tyler: Wait—I have so many questions for you.

Rennon: We can't just leave!

Declan: Do not worry. We will meet again.

Nymbus: REMEMBER, THE ONE WHO SEEKS TRUTH SHALL FIND IT, ALWAYS, AND LIKE THE PHOENIX, THE ROYALS SHALL RISE AGAIN.

CHAPTER THIRTY-TWO
THE CHOICE

It was a knee-jerk reaction—a return to reality like being yanked by an invisible force in direct contrast to the smooth, peaceful drift into the realm. Tyler's eyes snapped open, gasping filling his lungs as he reached into the void before him. There was only the disorientation at first, a momentary cloak until the familiar contours of the study materialized around him, his fingers still intertwined with Diana's. Diana blinked her eyes open softly, and she released a sigh that rasped through the room. "I forgot to mention it was a bit rocky coming back," she said, her voice a calm anchor in the turbulent return.

Rennon came last, pulling breath deep into his lungs, mimicking Tyler. He jumped up, looking around the room before running a hand through his hair and turning to Tyler and Diana.

"Can we ever go back?" Tyler asked. He knew the chances were slight, given all that Nymbus shared, but he was hopeful anyway.

"Maybe one day. I don't know," Diana said, looking at Rennon and Tyler. As Tyler removed his glasses, a deep sigh came from within him. The travel into another realm sapped more of him than he had realized, more so than his efforts with the Tied Fruit. Putting his glasses back on, he felt no more pain from where his hand was previously bandaged. Curious, he unwrapped the cloth to see his wound closed altogether. "A benefit of your gifted blood," Diana explained, "You will both grow stronger with each day."

Rennon inspected his own healed hand with a chuckle. "I could get used to this." Their moment of discovery was suddenly interrupted by a voice echoing downstairs.

"Hello! Anyone home?"

It was Kyle. Tyler bolted from the room, his feet barely touching the steps as he descended. The entrance hall was a hive of activity: workers painting, polishing, and setting out furniture, restoring the manor to its former beauty. "I guess the cleanup has officially begun," Tyler said with an ironic smile as he watched the orchestrated chaos.

"Yeah, no kidding," Kyle said in a dry tone.

Tyler stopped on the stairs, a frown beginning. "Back so soon? How's your mom?"

Kyle was puzzled.

"Uh, it's been like eight hours, Ty. She's good, a bit worried, but good." The truth hit Tyler harder than the first glance of reality back in this realm.

"Eight hours?" Tyler questioned. Diana and Rennon were on the stairs with him.

"Yes. Time moves differently there, too," Diana agreed.

"It seemed as though a few minutes. An hour maximum." Rennon said from the side, sidestepping a worker carrying a heavy chair when he reached the landing.

Kyle leaned in, cupping his mouth. "How was it?"

Tyler exhaled, his eyes wide with residual awe. "Overwhelming," he summed up.

As they began toward the kitchen, Rennon slung an arm around Kyle's shoulders, a sly grin stretching his lips. "If I had to choose one word, it'd be awesome," he said, laughing and rolling his eyes as Tyler watched, unable to keep a smile off his face. The camaraderie was something you could almost touch, up and down like everything else in life. As they entered the bunker, the entire energy in the room changed. It was all business. Caleb and Kodi were pouring over the information on the wall of monitors when James came out with Cassandra.

She dropped to one knee immediately.

"I should apologize again for my behavior—and baring my fangs—it won't happen again." Her apology was sincere.

Rennon helped her to her feet, his tone soothing. "Casi, it's alright."

"I'm glad you're all okay," James said, kissing Diana again.

"How was it?" Caleb asked.

"What an honor to meet an ancestor," Cassandra added.

Tyler: I don't want to tell them.

Tyler and Rennon nodded. The discoveries of the Astral Realm lingered unspoken as the thorn of mistrust pricked at Tyler's side once more, the weight of their experiences a shared but unsaid bond. Tyler wasn't sure if Diana could still read his thoughts as she dispelled the tension, taking a leather-bound journal from the shelves and giving it to Tyler. "You've read so much about others' journeys. Well, maybe it's about time you started writing your own."

Taking the journal into his hands, Tyler felt like he was drowning in purpose. "Thanks, Diana," he said, the journal's weight in his hands holding him at that moment. This was his story, meant to be inscribed on the pages of time and memory like those before him.

***

Entry 1:

It's almost three weeks since our trip to the Astral Realm, yet the echo of that place still lingers in my mind. James is convinced that the Cerif will not return to this realm again. He thinks they are conspiring to plan something even worse. Their threat makes it all the more necessary for me to grow stronger. I find it increasingly hard to balance creating the Tied Fruit for the Shafeir. Rennon, however, always so full of himself, tried to imitate the ritual himself when we got back, showing off by mimicking Nymbus' chant: "Fi—Vi—Di—tied in three."

It worked, of course. The fruit that he held changed, imbued with power. That launched a competition between us. I couldn't stand to let Rennon one-up me—we tried changing everything from oranges to apples and peaches into the Tied Fruit. Kyle joined in, taking out any fruit he could find. James sat by in amazement, commenting on how natural we were making the process look, which was once a long, drawn-out affair. But it wasn't without its drawbacks; Rennon and I could only do four successful Tied Fruit: presents for James, Cassandra—to ease her bloodlust—and the Scotler twins. We need the Shafeir at their peak if the Cerif decides to show their faces again. Meanwhile, the desire for normalcy—a semblance of the home I once knew— grew stronger. With Cassandra and Rennon moving into the manor, even its vast halls felt constricted…

"Tyler! Are you almost ready? Graduation is about to start, and we can't miss Kyle's speech," Rebecca's voice cut from downstairs. Tyler snapped the journal shut, his fingers lingering on the cover as he stood. Today was the giant first step in the return to normalcy—graduation day. He grabbed his cap and gown, descending the stairs where Rebecca and Rion waited, anticipation bright in their eyes. "You're not going to put on your gown now?" Rebecca's brow arched as she eyed Tyler's casual attire.

Tyler shook his head, "I'll change when we get there. I'm meeting up with Kyle first."

"All right, but let's hurry," Rebecca urged, opening the door to a day that felt like a dream. Her excitement seemed to overshadow Tyler's; a feeling of wishful thinking engulfed him that he had been able to make one more Tied Fruit for her to regain all those years and more. Once in the car, Tyler's fingers itched to be writing again; the pen hovered over the page like a siren song calling him back to his thoughts.

…Today's the day. It feels surreal to be here, at high school

graduation, after everything that has happened. I never thought I'd ever keep a diary, yet…here I am. Diana was right; recording my journey was critical—therapeutic, even. I owe her—and Rennon—more thanks than I can ever express. My brother—my twin—won't be with me today, but our bond remains.

Tyler was lost in thought and only vaguely aware of the passing landscape as he stopped writing, thinking of Rennon's absence.

Rennon: I'm still around, little brother.

Tyler: Little? How do you figure? I could've been born first.

Rennon: Just a feeling.

Tyler chuckled, returning to his journal.

…I'll have to remember to ask Rebecca and Casi who was born first. Rennon seems to believe I'm willfully blocking him out of the journal on purpose. Truthfully, there's something about this journal, like the Book of Vim and its disappearing ink, that keeps him from hearing my thoughts when I write. In a way, it's comforting to have a space just for myself.

The stop of the car in front of the school brought Tyler back to his senses. "We're here," Rebecca called, winking at him in the rearview mirror. Tyler shoved the journal into his backpack, picked up his cap and gown, and exited the car into the hectic buzz of graduation day. "Go on, go find Kyle, we'll catch up." Tyler grinned, closing the door.

"I love you both, thank you!" he continued, turning to the school's entrance. Inside, it was no different. The halls were filled with graduating students. Tyler could see Kyle waving by the auditorium and started to walk faster.

"You haven't gotten dressed yet?" Kyle asked, a hint of panic in his tone as he glanced toward the auditorium where students began assembling.

"I figured there'd be time here," Tyler replied, rushing toward the nearby dressing rooms. "I'll be quick!" he shouted, ducking into the room to pull his gown over his clothes in the mirror. Tyler was met with an unexpected presence as he struggled with the cap and gown.

"Need a hand?" A calm voice said.

"Who's there?" Tyler asked, finally pulling the gown over his head to see a young man about his age standing behind him with an urgent expression, holding Tyler's cap.

"Tyler, there isn't much time," his eyes nervously scanned the room as he thrusted the cap into Tyler's hands. "My name is Phoenix. I've come to warn you about what's coming."

"Phoenix?" Tyler said. Disbelief washed over his mind—the name matching that of the author of the articles on the Shafeir that he had read, from an author who apparently should have been dead. "How do you know who I am?"

"Listen, where is the book?" he pressed, urgency threading his voice.

What book? Tyler was going to say, but the announcement of the beginning of the ceremony broke through the words. "I've got to go," he said before turning to run out and join the procession, but even after he left the room, Phoenix's warning sat heavily on Tyler's mind as he ran down the now-empty halls. He took his place in line with the other students headed into the auditorium. The large room seemed to warp. The principal started the ceremony by welcoming everyone.

"Thank you all for being here today. We are very excited for this year's graduates."

A peculiar sensation crept over Tyler as the principal spoke. He sat in his seat, anxiously awaiting Kyle's speech. The fabric of reality began to thin. It was a familiar event to Tyler's experience in his classroom months ago. His heart quickened, the ring pulsating on his finger. Tyler's vision started to blur and then darken, and from his seat in the auditorium at his high school graduation, his world fell away.

From darkness to blaring wind, Tyler suddenly found himself no longer seated in the auditorium but soaring through strangely familiar surroundings. Ascending and diving below the skyline. Feathered wings—majestic and white—carried him high above breathtaking landscapes, rivers weaving through the twilight like threads of silver. He skimmed the surface of a mirror-like lake only to ascend sharply along the rugged face of a towering castle. Coming to a sinister figure with piercing red eyes at the top, their gazes locked—suddenly, an invisible force yanked him from the sky.

Plummeting into an abyss, he struggled desperately to regain his flight, but his wings were no more. Voices flooded into the nightmare, pulling Tyler back to the auditorium.

"Tyler Asoron. Is Tyler here?" The announcer's voice echoed faintly as a student nudged him, noticing his distress. As Tyler blinked away the vision, the ground beneath him began to tremble.

What started as a minor shake soon became a violent rumble, sending panic through the auditorium. Students and guests screamed, bolting from their seats as the tremor intensified. Tyler scanned the chaos for Kyle, Rebecca, and Rion, but they were nowhere to be found.

"Kyle!" Tyler shouted over the chaos, but there was no answer. The auditorium groaned and swayed, banners falling and lights flickering wildly.

Tyler: Rennon! Help!

Tyler's mental plea went unanswered. Fueled by the fleeing crowd, Tyler made his way out and was bombarded by questions and fears. What's going on? Why now? He stumbled down the steps outside, falling as the quake suddenly stopped, leaving a scene of destruction. Car alarms wailed. Streetlights lay broken and uprooted from the ground, smashing cars. Parts of the building crumbled.

Was this the disaster Phoenix warned him about? Dust caked his gown as he crawled on the ground, Kyle exploding through the doors to the auditorium, the limp body of a girl clutched tight to his chest. "Ky!" Tyler shouted as he dropped to his knees beside him. They eased the girl onto the pavement. "What's going on?" Tyler demanded, full of fear.

Kyle shook his head, a worried look all over his face. "She's alive, but the others, we need to find help." At that moment, a woman's scream split the air. She rushed toward them, tears pouring out of her eyes, likely the girl's relative, and embraced the girl in her arms, shouting out frantically for help.

"We have to find my—" Tyler started.

The sound of sirens in the distance cut him off. Kyle turned to him with a grim expression. "We need to get out of here. That quake wasn't natural," he said, gripping his amulet with finality. Nodding somberly, he spoke the word to activate the amulet.

"Prokimos, O Alexos!"

His form instantly shifted, and he transformed into the winged guardian Aleks. In one fluid motion, Aleks lifted Tyler into the sky. The ground receded rapidly, the chaos shrinking into a distant blur. Numb with shock and in the grasp of Aleks, Tyler's mind raced. He reassured himself that his aunt and uncle were safe; they had to be. As they rose into the sky, Tyler found himself staring at the unknown before him once more, Phoenix's warning weighing heavy on his heart. Whatever was to come, he was prepared to face it.

THE END

TYLER WILL RETURN.

EPILOGUE

THE PROSPECTIVE FUTURE

Entry 79:

The bitter cold nights are taking their toll on me in this place. I try to keep count of the passing moonlit nights, but frankly, I've lost track of time altogether—perhaps three or four now. It's so dark here. I see no sunlight during what I feel like is day, and I feel the biting cold of what I can only describe as night. The passing moons above my head are the only light in this forsaken dark as I lay against the damp, stone walls in this cylindrical space. My journal, this pen, and the chains are my only comfort against the dim warmth of the single torchlit flame.

I can hear the voices above me, whispers, and footsteps. Guards, Shafeir travelers from the Mirror Realms, waiting for me to lose control again. They believe me to be insane. I pleaded with James before my confinement. That man and his magic, he did this to me. Binding my connection to the ancestors. Curse them.

It was only a momentary lapse, an accident, but none of them believed me, not even my brother. What more do they want? What more can I give to them? Fear has settled in them now, thinking I'm like the ones before me. This was all a mistake. Coming here was a mistake.

I don't hear Ren anymore. His voice has quieted over time, and something else calls to me now—faint whispers from the depths—darkness. Where is my family? Where is Kyle?

They told us we were royalty, powerful descendants meant to rule and protect, but who protected us from them? What stolen power were we meant to wield? Curse them...

The torch flickered in Tyler's eyes, casting long, wavering shadows on the cold stone walls. Tyler shivered, hugging his knees to his chest. The dampness seeping into his bones, he could barely remember the warmth of sunlight on his skin. Memories of the moment he was dragged away rang in his head. "James, you have to believe me. It was an accident," he said, desperation in his voice. James had looked at him with sorrow and fear.

"This is beyond our understanding…you need to be contained, for everyone's sake." He replied. His words were like a knife to Tyler's chest. Tears filled his eyes as they dragged him away.

"James, it was the Magi! That man, he did this to me!" But his pleas had fallen on deaf ears, and now he was alone in this dark, cold prison. A noise from beyond snaps Tyler out of his thoughts. As if a radio was being tuned for clear transmission to his ears.

Tyler: I thought you were gone.

Rennon: I am, in a way. But I had to warn you.

Tyler: Warn me? Like Phoenix did?

Rennon: The whispers are not what they seem. They will try to deceive you—stay strong.

Tyler: Where are you? Where is Kyle? What have you heard?

There was silence again, leaving Tyler alone once more. The darkness pressing in, Tyler held on to Rennon's words, clinging to the fragile thread of hope, determined to reclaim what was his.

***

Originating from the bustling state of Utah, **T. J. SMITH** is a self-taught designer, artist, and author passionate about storytelling. Believing that the gift of storytelling cannot be ignored, T. J. brings to life a diverse and colorful fantasy universe, first conceived in a middle school classroom. These stories, born from simple lines of thought, explore different perspectives, experiences, and interconnected destinies, mirroring the complexity of our waking world.